Introduction

When I wrote "The Epic of Baal the God of Thunder," I conceived it as an illustrated book similar to my book "The Ennead." This book is the companion volume of "The Epic of Baal the God of Thunder." It contains an alternate and expanded version of the story of Canaanite mythology than that found in the previous book that I wrote, the illustrations I made, and different and shorter commentary. In oral cultures, it is common for there to be divergent versions of a myth and myths often changed over time, with many retellings.

This is an artistic exploration of Canaanite myth. I have used creative license mostly to create a narrative flow and to fill in the gaps of fragmentary stories. Scholars estimate that 50% of the text is missing from the tablets in Ugaritic that tell the story of the "Baal Cycle.' While this version of the story is shaped by my imagination, in reading it you will gain a basic accurate understanding of Canaanite myth. Scholarly works containing what is currently thought to be factual information about Cananite mythology are listed in the bibliography. (That being said, almost all of what is in this story is derived from the Ugaritic texts, Sanchuniathon, the Holy Bible and other ancient sources.) If reading this book sparks your curiosity and you would like to learn more and see what current scholarly consensus is on these stories and read direct translations of the Ugaritic texts that record these tales, I recommend that you consult the books listed in the bibliography.

In this story God is called El and Elohim. (In Hebrew Elohim is plural and in certain passages in the Bible means "gods." Elohim is usually used in the Bible as a name of God.) In this story, El represents the Canaanite conception of God and neither the modern nor Biblical conception of who God is. However, some of the ancient Israelites shared this conception of God with the Canaanites.

Baal, Ashtoreth, Dagon, Molech and Asherah are Canaanite gods who are frequently mentioned in the Holy Bible. Who did the Canaanites believe these gods to be? Why did Israelites make idols of Golden Calves? What was an "Asherah Pole"? What were the "pagan ways" that the prophets of the Lord warned the Israelites not to emulate? Knowing the answers to these questions can deepen one's understanding of the Holy Bible. In 1929 important texts were discovered at Ras Shamra in Syria that told the story of the Canaanite gods. These Ugaritic texts, along with other ancient sources, help us to reconstruct the beliefs of the ancient Canaanites and widen our understanding of the Sacred Scriptures. This book is an illustrated version and extended edition of the story of the "Epic of Baal the God of Thunder."

I began this project as an attempt to understand Moses and the cultures that he emerged from. He was raised as an Egyptian and as a Hebrew. It needs to be understood that the two cultures that Moses grew up in-that of Egypt and of the Semitic settlers in Egypt, were both pagan cultures.

The Bible is very clear about this. According to the Bible, while the Hebrews were slaves in Egypt, they worshiped gods in Egypt (Joshua 24:14, Ezekiel 20:7-8). They had no knowledge of the name of God (Exodus 3:13-14, 6:2-3). God first revealed himself to the Israelites in Egypt through Moses (Exodus 4:30-31). In many places in the Bible it is stated that God (Yahweh or

"Jehovah") first revealed himself to Israel when they were slaves in Egypt (1 Samuel 2:27, Ezekiel 20:5, Hosea 11:1, 12:9, 13:4). The Hebrews did worship God as El Shaddai but Moses revealed the name of Yahweh to them. Exodus 6:3 says, "And I appeared unto Abraham, unto Isaac, and unto Jacob, by the name of **God Almighty [El Shaddai]**, but by my name Jehovah was I not known to them." Moses said the Yahweh, "Behold, when I come unto the children of Israel, and shall say unto them, The God of your fathers hath sent me unto you; and they shall say to me, What is his name? what shall I say unto them?" (Exodus 3:13). What this likely means it, "Which of the gods of our fathers is sending you to us?"

In Joshua 24:14, Joshua says, "Now therefore fear the LORD [YAHWEH], and serve him in sincerity and in truth: and put away the gods which your fathers served on the other side of the flood, and in Egypt; and serve ye the LORD." This is evident that the Israelites were worshiping many gods in Egypt.

Ezekiel 20:7-8, "And say unto them, Thus saith the Lord GOD; In the day when I chose Israel, and lifted up mine hand unto the seed of the house of Jacob, and made myself known unto them in the land of Egypt, when I lifted up mine hand unto them, saying, I am the LORD [YAHWEH] your God; In the day that I lifted up mine hand unto them, to bring them forth of the land of Egypt into a land that I had espied for them, flowing with milk and honey, which is the glory of all lands: Then said I unto them, Cast ye away every man the abominations of his eyes, and defile not yourselves with the idols of Egypt: I am the LORD your God. But they rebelled against me, and would not hearken unto me: they did not every man cast away the abominations of their eyes, neither did they forsake the idols of Egypt: then I said, I will pour out my fury upon them, to accomplish my anger against them in the midst of the land of Egypt." This Scripture says that Yahweh God revealed Himself to the Israelites in Egypt before the Exodus. While in Egypt, Yahweh tells them to put away the gods that they are worshiping. They do not, even after the Exodus and the Conquest of the Holy Land.

The question now is, what gods were the Israelites worshiping in Egypt? Where they worshiping Egyptian gods? I am sure that they were to an extent. But it is obvious that they were worshiping the Canaanite gods during their sojourn in Egypt. (In is interesting that, centuries later, after the Babylonian Captivity, a Jewish community returned to Egypt. This was probably part of the group that forcibly took the Prophet Jeremiah to Egypt. In Egypt, Jeremiah rebukes them for their continuing to worship the Queen of Heaven (probably Asherah). They answered Jeremiah that the worship of Asherah was a long established Jewish tradition. Archeologists have found Aramaic texts in Elephantine in Egypt, where we find the Jewish community of Egypt devoted to the worship of Yahu (Yahweh) and to Anath-whom they viewed as his wife.

There was a large community of Semitic settlers in Egypt. These settlers were sometimes called "Hapiru," "Asiatics," and "Syrians." We see in the Bible, and in Egyptian sources, Semitic settlers in Egypt rising to high position in Egyptian government. The Bible tells of Joseph becoming an Egyptian dignitary and in Egyptian sources we learn of an Aper-el, who was a vizier of Pharaoh Akhenaten. There were so many Semites in Egypt that these people began to have a strong influence on Egyptian culture. Semitic slaves in Egypt were probably the inventors

The Baal Cycle:
The Art of the Epic of Baal

By
Stephen Andrew Missick

of the alphabet that we use today. This shows that their cultural influence isn't restricted to ancient Egypt but is impacting us today. The cultural influence of Semitic settlers in Egypt was so great that the Egyptian began worshiping Semitic gods. (Also, for a while these Semites actually ruled over Egypt as Pharaohs in the Hyksos Dynasty.)

Semitic gods worshiped in Egypt includes Baal, Anath, Resheph, Horon, Ashtoreth (Astarte) and Qudshu (probably Asherah). It is possible that Pharaoh Rameses the Great may have been of Semitic descent himself. He praises Baal in his inscriptions and named one of his daughters Bint-Anath, meaning "Daughter of Anath."

So, in order to understand Israelite culture during their Egyptian Sojourn it is important to understand Canaanite mythology. In the Exodus account, we find the Israelites camping at "Baal Zaphon," (Exodus 14:2-4) this was a place in Egypt named after Baal's holy mountain in Syria. However, this isn't only important in studying the Exodus, but the entirely of the Old Testament. As I have mentioned, we see the Israelites still worshiping the Canaanite gods during the time of the Prophet Jeremiah and afterwards. This is also the cultural background to the story of the Prophet Elijah and his conflict with King Ahab and Queen Jezebel. The Bible judges whether a king was successful or not based upon how he advocated the worship of Yahweh and repressed the Canaanite religion.

Therefore we see that it is important to have a working knowledge of Canaanite mythology in order to properly understand the cultural context of many of these Bible stories.

The Canaanite Pantheon:

El: El is the Creator of the Universe and the Father of the gods. He is described as being "merciful and compassionate." He fathered the gods and goddesses through his wife, the goddess Asherah. He is described as the "Bull El." The Bull was his symbol because the ancients looked upon Bull's as being a symbol of strength and fertility. El is also described as dwelling in a tent. The "Golden Calf" was most likely viewed by the Israelites as a symbol of El. El is a pagan god, but his name is used as one of the names of God in the Holy Bible.

Asherah: Asherah was a mother goddess and the wife of El. She was the mother of the "Seventy Sons of El" who were the gods of the ancient Canaanites. A tree was used to symbolize Asherah.

Dagon: Dagan was a god of grain. Long after his worship died out, the rabbis wrongly assumed that Dagan was a fish god because his name sounds like a Hebrew word for fish.

Baal: Baal means "lord" and is used as a word for husband in Modern Israeli Hebrew. Many different gods were called Baal. In the Ugaritic texts, Haddad, the god of rain and thunder, is often referred to as Baal.

Molech: The name Molech means "King." The Milcom worshiped by the Ammonites may have been the spirits of their former kings. An underworld god named Athtar may have been Molech.

Ashtoreth: Ashtoreth is Astarte and Ishtar. She is a sex goddess. She was similar to the Greek god Aphrodite and the Roman god Venus. Some scholars believe that after a time her worship merged with that of Asherah and Asherah and Ashtoreth became fused together as the same goddess in the minds of their adherents. However, the biblical Ashtoreth should not be confused with the goddess Asherah, the form of the names being quite distinct, and both appearing quite distinctly in the Book of 1st Kings.

Shamash: Shamash is the Hebrew word for "sun" and Shamash was also a sun-god in Semitic mythology. In Ugarit, the sun is a goddess called Shapash.

Yerikh: Yerikh is the Hebrew word for "moon." Yerikh is also a Canaanite god whose name is referenced in the city of Jericho.

Meth: This god is also called Mot and Mot is the Hebrew word for "Death." Meth is the god of death.

El/Baal Berith: According to the Book of Judges, the Israelites of Shechem had built a temple to El/Baal Berith-the lord, or god, of covenants.

Anath: Anath was a warrior goddess. In the book of Judges, the judge Shamgar is described as being a "Son of Anath." Jeremiah came from the city of Anathoth, a city named after Anath.

Resheph: Resheph is the Hebrew word for plague and the name of the Canaanite plague god. Resheph was also worshiped in Egypt.

(A more detailed glossary of the Canaanite gods is found in the back of this book.)

The prophets of the Lord struggled against Canaanite mythology for centuries before they were able to bring the Israelites into the true understanding of who God really is. It seems that it was only after the Babylonian Captivity that the Jews finally abandoned Canaanite beliefs and ideology and accept Yahweh as the one and only true God and the Creator of the Universe.

This is the symbol of the goddess Tanit and was used by the Canaanites, Phoenicians, and Carthaginians as a symbol of their religion, similar to the way Jews use the Star of David, Christians use the Cross and Muslims use the Crescent Moon.

The Epic of Baal the God of Thunder

The Baal Cycle Part One

ELOHIM

ELOHIM

Elohim creates the world and all life within it

In the name of *El Elyon*, the God Most High, the compassionate, the merciful, the Lord of Creation and the Ancient of Days. *El Elyon* is called *El Shaddai*, God Almighty. (The name *El* means "God." *El* is God. El is also called Elohim.) El, the King of the Universe, created the heavens and the earth and all that dwells therein. He is *Baal Shamayim*, which means, the Lord of Heaven. (The word Baal means "Lord.")

In the beginning El created the heaven and the earth. He is the Supreme Being and the Creator of the Universe and all that is seen and unseen.

At the start of all things *El Elyon*, the God Most High, stood upon the waters of chaos. All was formless void. And El created an expanse to separate the waters above the sky from the waters below the sky. This expanse was the open vault of the sky. The *tannim* dragon, a chaos demon named Rahab, that vile and twisting serpent, desired to rule in chaos and resisted God and the establishment of order. *El Elyon* fought her with the strength of a mighty bull. As his first act, God created the seed of wisdom. He held the seed in the palm of his hand and communed with her. Looking into the future, he saw what he must do and he saw that the seed of wisdom would return again to him in time. He gently blew upon the seed and it softly landed upon the chaotic waves where it was set adrift. El then created the Staff of God and his sword. With them he smote the Rahab. (Due to his strength and virility, a young bull is used as a symbol of God and his power.) Finally, he tore Rahab asunder. By his power he stilled the waters; by his wisdom he cut Rahab to pieces. By his breath, he cleared the sky, by his hand he crushed the twisting serpent. Two creatures emerged from within her body and were born of her as she was ripped in two. El Elyon threw her body down and it became as dry land. Rahab's son Leviathan swam into the waters to dwell. Her other son, Behemoth, went to dwell on the dry land, formed from his mother's carcass. Leviathan and Behemoth fought against Elohim. God subdued both of these creatures but spared their lives. Behemoth fled from God and hid in the mountains and in the caves. And God then stilled the raging waters of chaos. El used the magic power of his staff to calm and divide the waters. Putting a hook in the mouth of Leviathan the unruly sea-serpent, El tamed Leviathan and called him Yam the Dragon of the Sea. He subdued Yam and shut the sea behind bars and doors and created a boundary for it and commanded Yam the sea, "Here you shall go and no further." He conquered the Leviathan and gave him the name Yam, meaning Sea, and allowed him to rule the seas under His authority.

El slaughters Rahab the Chaos Demon

El creates the vault of the sky over the earth-which he formed from the corpse of Rahab.

God laid the foundation of the earth. He marked out its dimensions and stretched a measuring line across the earth. He set the earth's foundations and it's cornerstones. He created the oceans and the springs that abound with water. He settled the mountains in place and secured the fountains of the deep. And El took what had been the breasts of Rahab and established them as mountains that securely hold up the firmament that he created. These twin peaks were called Targhizizi and Tharumagi, which hold the sky up above the earth-circling ocean, thereby bounding the earth. These mountains, at the far corners of the earth, both have entrances to the underworld within them. He set the heavens in place and established the clouds above. He marked out the horizon upon the face of the deep.

El walked along the surface of the world that he had created

God walked alone upon the surface of the earth that he created. As He walked along the shore and he looked and saw an object bobbing up and down as it floated upon the waters. It washed ashore. El came upon it and lifted it up. It was a seed. He took it and planted it upon the earth. Suddenly, a tree grew up from the seed upon the surface of the earth. This was the first tree, the Tree of Life. It was the goddess Asherah (she is *Elath*-the goddess and is the Queen of Heaven). Asherah is also called *Qudshu* or *Qedeshet*, meaning "the Holy One." God saw the Tree of Life that it was beautiful. The spirit of Asherah emerged from the tree and assumed the form of a woman, perfect in beauty. (Asherah is the Tree of Life. Although she assumed a human form, the Tree is the extension of her being. She is the Sacred Grove. She can assume the form of a tree at will and she can merge again with the original Tree of Life at will. Her human form is that of a naked woman. She is the Naked Goddess of Heaven and Earth and *Hawa*, the Great Life and the Mother of All Living. She stood naked but she was not ashamed. Asherah is the source and the giver of the Water of Life. Asherah is also called *Peniel*, meaning "the Face of God." She is the Tree of Life and the Tree of Knowledge. Her fruit imparts wisdom and her leaves healing. All trees derive from Asherah.) El made love to Asherah. She gave birth to *Shachar* ("Dawn" or "the Morning") and *Shalim* ("Dusk"). God gave orders to the Morning and assigned Dawn to his place.

Asherah the Tree of Life

Asherah nurses Shachar and Shalim

Then El lay with her again and she gave birth to a son, *Shamash*, the god of the Sun, and *Lillith*, the mistress of the night. And Elohim created a helpmate for Shamash from Shamash's own body and he named her Shapash. Shamash and Shapash were of one flesh and they represented the masculine and feminine aspects of the Sun. And God created a chariot of fire drawn by six flying horses and gave it to Shamash that it may carry him across the sky far above the surface of the earth that his light may shine upon all the earth. The sky became as a tabernacle for the Sun. And Shalim took his place before the night. Then it was the first day. And God gave the day to the sun for him to rule over it. God established the rising of Shamash and the going down thereof and created a corridor through the Netherworld for Shamash to journey through that he may arise following Shachar.

Shamash drives his Chariot of Fire across the sky

Lillith (scholars do not agree which goddess is depicted in this image)

That first evening, El and Asherah produced another son, *Yerikh*, the moon. And he ruled over the night. The next day, El and Asherah had another son, Dagon, the god of vegetation. Dagon settled upon Mount Hammon and was known as *Baal Hammon*, meaning the Lord of Hammon. And then the earth brought forth vegetation and plants bearing seed and fruit trees of every kind. El created the earth's features. As he did the work of creation, Lady Asherah walked beside him and whispered words of wisdom and wise counsel into his ears. He created the springs of the sea and the recesses of the deep. And Elohim created the fish of the sea, the birds of the air, cattle, and all kinds of animals and all the creeping things of the earth.

And the Behemoth emerged from his hiding place and began to eat all the living things that God had made. Behemoth opened his mouth so wide that it seemed to extend from the earth to the sky. The Behemoth aimed to kill everything that God gave life to. And so El restrained Behemoth, so that life may endure. He tamed him and made him stand as a god and gave him the name Enoch, but the Behemoth called himself Meth, meaning "Death." And so, God restrained Meth so that life may endure but he gave him a place in the cosmic order.

El lay with Asherah and she conceived and bore a daughter in her exact image. She named her Tanith. Dagon loved his sister and made her his wife. Tanith then was called *pene baal* meaning the "face of Baal" and "Rabat," which means "female chieftan." And Tanith (who is also known as Tanit) approached her father and made a request of him. "Give me children," she asked. "I shall give you children," he answered her, "but the children of Dagon will be counted as my own." And he lay with her and she conceived and bore triplets. Her first born was a son who was named Haddad. He is the God of Thunder and he gave rain to water the face of the earth. Haddad had two sisters- Anath and Ashtoreth. Anath and Ashtoreth were identical twins. Anath became the goddess of sexual love and warfare and Ashtoreth became the goddess of lust, lovemaking, beauty and military pomp. While they were identical in appearance as they grew older the differences between their personalities became more pronounced. Anath was fierce, courageous and passionate while Ashtoreth became vain, fickle, temperamental and self-centered. God then created storehouses for hail and snow and created a path for the thunderstorm, where Baal Haddad could exercise his power. Haddad is Baal the god of thunder.

Tanith

Dagan-the Lord of Hammon

Anath in an image from Ancient Egypt-where she was worshiped

And again El lay with Asherah and Asherah then gave birth to Sheol, the goddess of the afterlife, who ruled the regions under the earth. And God saw that Sheol was a creature of darkness and that she despised the light and life. And God sought a dwelling place for her, a place where light is withheld. He then entered into the springs of the sea in the realms beneath the earth and he walked in the search of the deep. There in the abode of darkness, slime, mire and phlegm, a miry pit, he created the realm of Sheol, and a place for his daughter Hell (Sheol) to dwell. He created seven levels in Hell, each one deeper than the other. He formed seven gates, which he gave to Meth as an abode. The gates confined Sheol to the Netherworld. The deepest pit in Hell is where Sheol sat upon her throne and ruled her kingdom. The gates of death were opened up before God and he gazed within the doors of the shadow of death. God perceived all that is above, within and beneath the earth. He perceived the breadth of all creation. And so God created the realm of Sheol, the Netherworld, and the Gates of Death. Sheol was imprisoned within the realm El created for her as a domain for her to rule over as queen of the damned ruling with Meth within the deep places under the earth. Meth dwelt within the realm of Sheol as his abode but, unlike Sheol, he come and go as he pleased. In Aramaic, Sheol was called Shuwala.

In all, El and Asherah begat and gave birth to seventy gods and also goddesses. These divine beings were the children of El and Asherah and their descendents. Chief among the sons of God were Resheph, the god of pestilence and divine judgment, Athtar, the Morning Star, who was the god of war and the son of Shachar, the god of dawn. Also among the sons of God was Shamash, the Sun god and the god of justice, Dagon, the god of vegetation, Haddad, the god of the life-giving rain, Rahmay, the goddess of mercy, the Ashtoreth, who is also called Astarte and Ishtar, who is the goddess of lust, beauty and sexual pleasure, and Anath, the goddess of sex, devoted love, and warfare. Ashtoreth is also called Baalat meaning "the Lady." Notable among the sons of God was the craftsman of the gods. He had many names including Elisha and Kothar-wa-Khasis which means "Skillful and Wise." His dwelling place was Memphis in Egypt and there he was known as Ptah. The sons of God were called *Bene Elohim*. God assigned all of his children their place in the night sky as his heavenly host.

In the east El created the Mountain of God. This mountain is called Mount Laila, the Mountain of the Night. This Cosmic Mountain is located at the source of the two great rivers, the Tigris and Euphrates, and at the spring of two seas. At the base of this mountain is Eden, the Garden of God, where the Tree of Life was planted. God's throne is by the Tree of Life. God sits enthroned between two cherubim. The cherubs are winged sphinxes. God also created the wilderness in which he would dwell at times in his sacred tent as his dwelling place. And God also erected Mount Zaphon and built upon it a hall in which all of his children could come and hold counsil. Haddad was the favored son of El, who presided over El's divine assembly in his absence. El presides over all, including the counsel of the sons of God. El would, at times, delegate his authority to Baal. The divine assembly of the sons of Elohim held court on the northern side of Mount Zaphon. God has a throne in the highest heaven but he has his holy places upon the earth. In the realm above he dwells within a thick darkness. In Eden, He emits a marvelous light.

The Sacred Tent of El

And then God forged the Tablets of Destiny that determined the fate of men and the gods. He wore the Tablets upon his chest beneath his garments. With Yerikh the moon-god, he established a measurement for the days, and created the cycle of the moon, to divide the year into months. In truth, God created Yerikh the Moon for Mo'adim –the appointed times. So God created the phases of the Moon and gave Yerikh the ability to renew himself on the Day of the Renewal of Yerikh called Yom Khodesh, the day of the New Moon.

And so God completed his creating and he looked upon all that his hands had made and delighted in it and said, "It is good." And then the morning stars sang together, and all the sons of God shouted for joy, delighting and rejoicing in all that God had made.

The Anakin

And the gods worked the earth in order to find nourishment. The gods became weary from laboring upon the earth. And so they created mindless brutes to work for them. These brutes were called the Anakin. They were gigantic and mighty. After centuries of laboring for the gods, the Anakin revolted against the gods. They were led by Anak and were called the sons of Anak. (There were different castes among the Anakin. Anak belonged to the higher caste that had greater intellects. He had served as a foreman and had directed the Anakin in their labors for the gods. The Anakin had no knowledge of their parentage since their females, without shame, would have intercourse with any male whom they might chance to meet. These begat sons of vast bulk and height. They were all called the sons of Anak because he was the mightiest among them.) There was a great battle-the gods verses the Anakin. Anath, Lord Haddad, Reshep and Athtar led the gods in battle against the rebellious Anakin. And God looked upon the battle and saw that the Anakin were prevailing against the sons of God. Only Anath and Haddad were able to hold their ground, the other sons of God remained standing but they were losing ground. God then commanded all the gods to join Anath and the others in the fight against the Anakin hoards and El even commanded Ashtoreth to join in the battle. She was loath to do this as Ashtoreth was skilled in love-making and not war-fighting. Thus she went to Ptah and asked him to forge magical weapons for her to make her powerful in battle. Once she received enchanted armor and weapons from Ptah she joined the battle against the Anakin. All the host of heaven fought against the Anakin. The Anakin fled from before Anath and the other gods who fought at her side. The gods were victorious and vanquished the Anakin. The surviving Anakin dwelt in the dark places of the earth and in the underworld. Some of them became demonic spirits and others became the servants of Sheol and Meth. After the battle, Anath rewarded Resheph, Haddad and the others among the gods who fought most valiantly by sharing with them the pleasures of her love.

Anath battling the Anakim

Anak the leader of the Anakim

El Creates Mankind

Having been deprived of their slave labor, the gods again wearied themselves looking for sustenance. And the counsil of the gods gathered and said, "Let us make man in our image and in our likeness that he may work the earth and that he may sustain us with his worship and offerings."

And God had taken the Asherah tree and planted it eastward, in Eden at the Mountain of God. And there he took a pinch of earth and from it he fashioned men and women. In the image of God created he them, male and female created he him. And he placed them in the garden he created for them to dress and keep the Tree of Life, which was planted in the midst of the garden. And he called this garden "Eden." And God created a guardian for Asherah, a protective serpent named Nehushtan, that coiled himself around her branches and watched over her.

And El dwelt upon the Holy Mountain. He erected his tent at the source of the great river from which the Water of Life flowed. The Water of Life flows out of the base of the Tree of Life and is the gift of Asherah. She is the giver of the Water of Life. The Tree of Life grows in the Garden of Eden in the place called Harosheth, meaning the wooded heights.

The Asherah tree was as a cedar in Lebanon with beautiful branches, and with a forest shade, and of a towering stature; and her top was among the thick clouds. The nourishing waters, the water of life, made her great, the deep made her grow tall with her rivers running round about the place where she was planted, and which sent out streams unto all the trees of the field. Therefore her height was exalted above all the trees of the field, and her boughs were multiplied, and her branches became long because of the abundance of waters, in her shoots. All the birds of heaven made their nests in her boughs, and under her branches did all the beasts of the field bring forth their young, and under her shadow lived all the peoples of the earth. Thus she was fair in her greatness, in the length of her branches: for her root was by great waters. These were the waters that formed the great seas and divided into the mighty rivers. (And a river went out of Eden to water the garden; and from thence it was parted, and became into four heads. The name of the first is Pison: that is it which compasses the whole land of Havilah, where there is gold; and the gold of that land is good: there is bdellium and the onyx stone are there as well. And the name of the second river is Gihon: the same is it that flows around the whole land of Cush. And the name of the third river is Hiddekel, also called the Tigris: that is it which goes toward the east of Assyria. And the fourth river is Euphrates.) The cedars in the garden of God could not rival the Tree of Life, which was in the midst of the Garden: the fir trees were not like her boughs, and the chestnut trees were not like her branches; nor the oak or the terebinth nor any tree in the garden of God was like unto her in her beauty. El made her fair by the multitude of her branches: so that all the trees of Eden, that were in the garden of God, envied her.

Adam in the Garden of Eden

Man is Expulsed from the Garden of Eden

God created men and women from the dust of the earth. He created a perfect man to rule over the men and women that he had made. He called this man Adam and he was created as the signet of perfection, full of wisdom and perfect in beauty. He was blameless in his ways in the day he was created. He was placed in Eden, the Garden of El and there he would minister before El and fellowship with him. He was given a crown of beauty. His clothing was adorned with twelve precious stones Red Jasper, Topaz, Emerald, Ruby, Lapiz Lazuli, Diamond, Sapphire, Agate, Amethyst, Chrysolite, Onyx, and Chrysoprase—all beautifully crafted for him and set in the finest gold upon a breastplate. This garment was called the Ephod and was patterned after the Tablets of Destiny. A cherub, a winged sphinx, was given to the man to guard him in Eden. Adam had access to the holy mountain of God and he walked among the stones of fire. (The stones of fire were huge chunks of incense that burned before the Lord and emitted a sweet smelling scent.) For several centuries, Adam served before El in the Garden of Eden and at the Mountain of God with faithfulness. And yet after many years had passed, his heart became proud because of his beauty and iniquity was found in him. He corrupted his wisdom for the sake of his splendor and he said, "I am a god. I shall sit in the seat of the gods." And so Adam approached the throne of God while El was away and took his seat upon it. He said within himself, "I will ascend into heaven, I will exalt my throne above the stars of God: I will sit also upon Mount Zaphon, the mount of the congregation of the gods, in the sides of the north: I will ascend above the heights of the clouds; I will be like the Most High." Later, El came into his Garden and discovered the man sitting upon the throne of God. In anger God spoke to the man he created, "You are a man and not a god and so you shall die as a man." But seeing the man cowering in fear, El felt compassion for him. Instead of destroying him, he stripped the man of his sacred garments, and exposed Adam's nakedness to his shame. He then cast out man as a profane thing from the Mountain of El and the guardian cherub that had been man's protector drove the man out of the Garden and from among the stones of fire. And God placed a Seraph, a fiery winged flying serpent, at the entrance of the garden, to spit out fiery poison at any mortal who would dare to attempt to enter, in order to prevent any human being from gaining access to the Tree of Life. Adam was then deprived from access to the Tree of Life and was thus condemned to mortality and condemned to struggle for his own survival in the wilderness, far from the presence of God. (Anyone who continually ate from the fruit of the Tree of Life could live forever. All those who die, good and evil, rich and poor, go to Sheol. The evil sink down into Sheol in despair. The righteous go into eternal rest but they can, if honored by the living, become awaken souls able to interact with the world of the living. These deified dead are called the Rephaim.) After the expulsion of man from Eden, mankind spread out upon the face of the earth. And man multiplied and filled the earth. At first men scavenged for food. Other men began hunting animals. Men then constructed reed huts and made clothing out of the skins of animals. Later, men discovered the secret of fire. Men began to fish and to create boats. Then they began planting crops. Finally, men began to keep sheep and cattle. Men began to build with stones and bricks. At times, gods would come down and instruct men and teach them the arts of civilization. A wise man who was a disciple of Ptah discovered how to forge metal. From Egypt, a servant of Thoth, the scribe of the gods, learned the art of writing. Years later, a man named Cadmus developed an alphabet and established a school for scribes. Men would worship the gods by offering sacrifices upon the high places and they worshiped Asherah at the sacred groves. Later, they built shrines to worship El, the gods and the Rephaim. However, men began to make weapons and used them to fight among themselves and there began to be wars.

A Cherub

A Seraph

Atrakhasis and the Great Flood

And the earth became filled with violence and their cries came up unto the gods and the gods were sore displeased. And the gods met at the divine counsel and they said, "Let us destroy man whom we have created from off the face of the earth." At first, the gods sent Resheph to wipe out mankind with a plague, but then a wise man named Atrakhasis, a servant of God, compelled the people to worship Resheph and Resheph was appeased by the peoples offering and sacrifices and he ceased the plague. When the plague ceased the people made Atrakhasis king. But then it was decreed that the gods would send a flood to destroy man from upon the face of the earth. But El is the Kindly One and the Merciful One, He loved mankind and sought for a way to save mankind from extinction. And El had favor upon Atrakhasis the righteous king. The people had named Athrakhasis king due to his kindness, wisdom and justice. And he appeared to Atrakhasis and commanded him to build an ark and place within it food and all manner of birds and animals, along with scribes and smiths and men skilled in crafts and the members of his own family. And Atrakhasis did so. After the door of the ark was closed a great flood came upon the earth and it rained for seven days and seven nights. The ark floated upon the waters and after the flood the ark came to rest in the mountains of Uratu. When the waters had assuaged from upon the face of the earth, Atrakhasis and all that were within the ark came out. And El appeared before them and said, "Be fruitful and multiply and replenish the earth."

Resheph-the plague god-from Ancient Egypt

Then Atrakhasis built an altar and offered up an ox that he had brought aboard the ark. He made horns upon the corners of the altar to honor the Bull El. He offered the ox up for a thanksgiving sacrifice to Elohim as a whole burnt offering. And the gods smelled the offering as a sweet aroma. They hovered around the offering and took sustenance from it. Then all the gods together swore an oath and said, "Let us never again send a flood to destroy all mankind; neither shall we again smite every living thing, as we have done."

The Ark of Atrakhasis

The Gods build cities among men

And again men spread out upon the earth. And some men settled in the east and there they built cities. The men of the east built towers that reached up into heaven upon which the sons of god descended to the earth and ascended again up to heaven. The name given to these towers was "Babel" meaning the Gate of El (Bab-El) or the gate of the gods. And the sons of god beheld the daughters of men that they were fair and they took wives from among them whomsoever they chose. And mighty men of valor were born to them. These demigods, who were half man and half god were called the Nephilim, because they were descended from those who had descended from heaven.

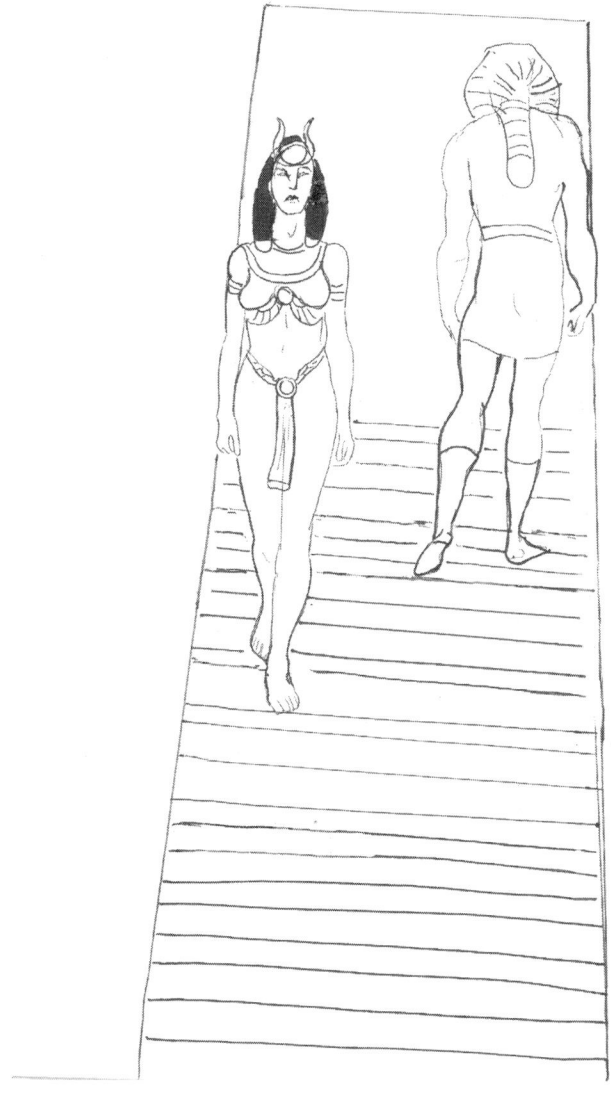

The Sons and Daughters of El ascending and descending the Bab-El

El Elyon apportioned the nations, he divided mankind. He fixed the boundaries of the peoples according to the number of the gods. He allotted a share to all the gods and granted them a portion of people to worship them. And cities were built upon the earth by the gods. El himself founded a city and it was named "Geb-el," which means "originated by El." Later, the city of Gebel was called Byblos, because books (*biblia*) were made there. El, the Goddess, and Reshep, the guardian of El were all worshiped at Gebel. There Asherah was called Baʻalat Gebal, meaning "the Lady of Gebal." Yerikh built the city Jericho (or "Yerikho") and named it after himself. (Yerikh was called Sin by the men of the east and he was honored in the land of Sinai and in Tayma.) Shalim who is called Zadok, the king of righteousness, also built a city that bore his name. He called his city Jeru-Shalim. Eshmoun, God of healing, was the eighth son of Zadok. He became the great god of Sidon. As he was the god of healing, he used the symbol of a serpent upon a pole to signify himself, since the snake rejuvenates himself when he sheds his skin. The pole also represents Asherah and the serpent her protector Nehushtan. Berith, the goddess of covenants, was given the city of Beirut. Later, Baal Hadad built the city of Tyre, where he was named Melqart (which means "King of the City"). He also built the city of Damascus where he was worshipped as Rimmon and the sacred pomegranate was his symbol. The goddess Anath had the cities of Anathoth and Beth-Anath built for herself. Asshur built his city which he named Nineveh. Murdock was given the city of Babylon by El. Qos, the Divine Archer, settled in Edom. Memphis was built by Kathor-wa-khasis. Chemosh was given rule over the plains of Moab. Amurru became the god of the Amorites. Carthage was given unto Tanith and Tarshish to Dagon and to Lady Asherah of the Sea to share. Men built the city of Beth-el, meaning "House of El," to honor God. (The sacred stone, which was also called Bethel and called Baetylus and Betyl by the Greeks, was set upon a pillar at Bethel. The Bethel Stone was given by God to mankind. El communicated with Mankind through the Bethel Stone often through dreams and visions that were transmitted through touching the Bethel Stone or by close proximity to it. The stone was a foot long and about half a foot wide.)The mermaid goddess Atargatis, called 'Atar'arah in Aramaic, was worshipped in Syria and in the city of Ascalon. Dagon, the Father of Baal, was worshiped in the five cities of the Philistines as well.

God also created the Watchers, called *Zopha Shamayim*, the Watchers, or Guardians, or Heaven, and they were called *Iyrin* in Aramaic. They observed the affairs of men and brought the prayers and intercession of men before God Most High.

One of the sons of Dagan and Tanith was Khirkhibi. He was the god of the summer months. He had a beautiful daughter that he named Nikkal. She was called *'Ilat 'Inbi*, or "Goddess of Fruit" and she was also called Nikkal-wa-Ib, meaning "Great Lady and Fruitful". Nikkal was the goddess of fruit and fertility. Yerikh, the moon god, saw her and desired her. Khirkhibi was reluctant to allow them to wed, and suggested that Yerikh instead wed the goddess Pidray or perhaps the goddess Yabarodmay. Yerikh refused, having set his sights on Nikkal alone. Yerikh paid Khirkhibi a bride-price of a thousand pieces of silver, ten thousand pieces of gold, and included necklaces made of lapis lazuli. Upon receiving this gift, Khirkhibi relented and allowed Yerikh and Nikkal to wed. Later, El sent seven of his daughters who were known as the

Kothirath, the "skillful goddesses" of marriage and childbirth, come to oversee the birth of the son of Nikkal and Yerikh. The Kothirath are the divine midwives and bless women in conception, in carrying a child and in giving birth. Yerikh blessed the Kothirath and named him as his own daughters and henceforth they were called the Radiant Daughters of the Crescent Moon. The son born to Yerikh and Nikkal was named Sheghar. Sheghar grew to be tall, strong and handsome. And Ashtoreth saw him and desired him. She seduced him and conceived and bore a son. She named him Hauron. Ashtoreth did not like to be encumbered on her sexual exploits with the burden of a child so when she thought that he was old enough to fend for himself, she abandoned him in the wilderness. There, life was a struggle and he almost died. But Hauron did survive and he became a mighty one. He became the lord of the desert places and became the god of those who herd goats, sheep, camels, donkeys, and cattle. He became a great warrior and was the god of all warriors-both the living and the dead. As such he also became a guardian of graves and tombs and the protector of the places of the dead.

Hauron

Yerich the Moon-god

Then arose one of the great kings. He was Eshmoun and was a mighty hunter before God. He called Eshmoun, meaning the Eighth, because he was the eighth son of Zadok. Eshmoun was tall, comely, strong, muscular and handsome. Eshmoun as a youth was fond of hunting. One day he returned from the hunt thirsty and weary. He came upon a well and saw a young woman there. He asked of her that she would give him a drink of water. As she gave him water to drink, he looked into her eyes and fell in love with her. He took this mortal woman named Astronoë to wife. He pledged himself to her that he would be faithful to her and love no other woman save her alone. One day as he was hunting, he was seen by the goddess Ashtoreth. She cast her eyes upon Eshmoun; and she said unto him, "Lay with me." But he refused, and said unto Ashtoreth, "How then can I do this great wickedness, and sin against Astronoë?" But Ashtoreth warned him, "I suffer no man whom I desire to refuse me." And it came to pass, as Ashtoreth spake to Eshmoun day by day, that he hearkened not unto her, to lie by her, or to be with her. When she pressed him daily with her words, and urged him, so that his soul was vexed unto death. And it came to pass after many days, that Ashtoreth found Eshmoun alone in the wilderness and she caught him by his garment, saying, "Lay with me." But he left his garment in her hand, and fled and ran. Having left the cloth that he wore over his naked body in her hand, he fled from her naked wearing only a belt that held his scabbard and sword. She pursued after him. As he ran, he glanced back and saw to his dismay that Ashtoreth was giving chase to him. He was dismayed when he realized that she ran faster than a cheetah and that she would soon overtake him. Ashtoreth harassed Eshmoun and pressed him so much with such amorous pursuit that in desperation he took his sword and he castrated himself and began to bled to death and fell unconscious. But Ashtoreth would not let such a beautiful man die. As he lay dying, Ashtoreth then took his shaft and reattached it to his body. He was by then cold and dead. But Ashtoreth restored him to life from the warmth of her body and she stimulated his body while he was unconscious and she made love to him; and he perceived not when she lay down, nor when she arose. And when he awoke, he knew it not. Ashtoreth by reviving Eshmoun had endowed him with the power to heal and she gave him the title of "Rafa," the 'Healer.' And thus, Eshmoun who had been the hunter and a taker of life became the god of healing and a giver of life. But Ashtoreth conceived and though her Eshmoun begat a daughter who was named Shataqat. She inherited the ability to heal from her father. The both of them discovered the healing herbs. Ashtoreth left Shataqat with Eshmoun and having had her desire fulfilled by Eshmoun sought out other men with which to satisfy her lusts. And Eshmoun founded the city of Sidon where he practiced and taught the art of healing. And lo, he became the great god of Sidon. Temples to Eshmoun were built in Carthage and elsewhere.

El Elyon, who is also called El Shaddai, also built a house of the gods upon Mount Zaphon where the gods would hold counsel. But, the dwelling place of El Elyon was a simple tent in the wilderness. And men built shrines under trees and upon the high places, temples, and sacred tabernacles with which to worship the gods. Sacred oaks and groves were set aside for the worship of Asherah. Men also made "Asherah-poles" which were stylized carvings of Ashtoreth-in either her human form or in the form of a stylized Tree of Life. Men also erected stone tablets and made carved images to symbolize the gods. And men sustained the gods through the giving of offerings and sacrifices of grain, produce, and bulls, heifers, goats and sheep. (But the unclean swine were not offered to the gods because they are not an acceptable sacrifice.) The offerings and sacrifices fed the gods.

Eshmoun

Shamash creates the Tablets of the Law

Now Shamash was the god of justice as well as being the god of the sun. As Shamash journeyed across the sky, he looked down and beheld mankind. And Shamash saw that the wickedness of man was great in the earth, he saw the innocent suffer and great injustice and it grieved him at his heart. In a night vision, Shamash appeared to King Amurapi, the ruler of the Amorites, in a dream. He commanded him to journey to a mountain that he would show him that he may give him commandments there. And King Amurapi did so. And it came to pass that the Amorite king found the mountain that Shamash had spoken of to him in a dream and he climbed to the top of the mountain and there Shamash appeared before Amurapi and gave him laws that the earth may have order and stability.

Shamash took a stone tablet and wrote his law upon it and erected it in a place that was frequented by the masses. As it was inscribed on stone, it could not be changed at the whim of man and it proclaimed immutable justice for all the people. He commanded Amurapi to make copies and erect them in every town in his kingdom that all people may have recourse to justice. And Amurapi did as he was commanded and erected the monoliths for his people.

And the law stated, "Whoever sheds the blood of a man, by the hand of man shall their blood be shed; for in the image of God has God made mankind. An eye for an eye, a tooth for a tooth. If a man puts out the eye of another man, put his own eye out. If he knocks out another man's tooth, knock out his own tooth. If he breaks another man's bone, break his own bone. If someone cuts down a tree on someone else's land, he will pay for it. If someone is careless when watering his fields, and he floods someone else's by accident, he will pay for the grain he has ruined. If a thief steals a cow, a sheep, a donkey, a pig, or a goat, he will pay ten times what it is worth. If he doesn't have any money to pay with, he shall become a servant until he has made amends or he will be put to death. If the son has done some great evil to his father, his father must forgive him the first time. But if he has done something evil twice, his father can throw him out. If a robber is caught breaking a hole into the house so that he can get in and steal, he can be put to death in front of that hole by the owner of the house. If a woman aborts her unborn child she shall surely be put to death. You shall not swear falsely, but you shall speak the truth." It contained sundry other laws. The law was engraved upon the stone tablet by the hand of Shamash.

Shamash gives the Amorite King his Law-code

The Tablet of the Law

The Wise King Daniel

And it came to pass in those days that there was a man named Daniel. He dwelt near to the land of Galilee. This Daniel was a man of great wisdom. Daniel was a just man, perfect and wise among his generation. He sat at the city gates and there he judged the cause of the widow and adjudicated the case of the fatherless. Due to his wisdom and sagacity he became recognized as a *Shophet*, also called a *suffete*, which is a judge. He gave a tithe of all of his possessions to the priests of El. The fame of his wisdom became widespread and many from nations far away came to hear the wisdom of Daniel. Daniel composed proverbs and collected knowledge. And yet, Daniel had no son. He gave all he had to help the poor and as offerings to the gods so that he lived with little wealth. Then Daniel built an altar to God. He built the altar of stones and made horns in its four corners to honor the Bull El. Daniel went up to worship God with offerings which were a sweet smelling aroma unto God. And he took of every clean bird and every clean animal and offered burnt offerings upon the altar. He slaughtered oxen, he killed sheep, bulls, fatling rams and yearling calves; he strangled lambs and kids. He gave Elohim ewes, bulls, and cows. He poured out wine as a drink offering to God. He ended his sacrifice with the offering of a goat kid. After he slaughtered the kid he boiled it upon the altar in its mother's milk. He made an offering for god to eat, he made sacrifices for the Holy One to drink. And Haddad saw the good works of Daniel.

Daniel offers up sacrifices to God.

And it came to pass, the sons of God appeared before Elohim and Baal was there among them. And so Haddad approached the Divine Assembly and spoke of the goodness of Daniel to the gods. But one of the sons of God, the Accuser, spoke derisively of Daniel and said, "Daniel is only a man and the heart of man is exceedingly wicked." Baal responded, "Daniel is a righteous man. Daniel possesses little but is great in wisdom, compassion and greatness of heart." And he said to God, "My father, El the Bull, won't you bless him? Oh, Creator of All, won't you show him your special favor?" El called Elisha before him and commanded him to bring Daniel to him. Suddenly, as Daniel walked along the side of the road, Kothar-wa-Khasis appeared before him. He spoke to Daniel, "Shalom! Peace be unto you. I am Ptah. I am called Elisha and Kothar-wa-Khasis, the Skillful and Wise. I have been sent to bring you into the presence of God." Elisha fell down before him as if dead. Ptah revived him and said, "Fear not, for you have found favor with God." Suddenly, Elisha grew so tall that his head reached into the clouds. He took up Daniel into his hand. Elisha carried Daniel to the mountain of God. With each step he would transverse a thousand fields, ten thousand acres with each step. As he carried him eastward towards the mountain of God, Ptah told Daniel how he must compose himself while in the presence of God. He told Daniel he must not eat food from off of the table of the gods but he must politely refuse it if it were offered to him.

Daniel beholds the glory of El

Daniel

Ptah-called "Kothar-wa-Khasis"- the skillful and wise

After many hours, they arrived at the mountain of God. As they prepared to enter into the Tabernacle, the Holy Tent of God, Ptah said unto Daniel, "Take the shoes from off of your feet, for the place upon which you stand is holy ground." And Daniel saw the Sea of Glass before the throne of God. The throne of God glowed brighter than the sun. A brilliant rainbow surrounded the throne. In front of the throne the stones of fire burned. To the right of the throne were torches burning with fire. At each side of the throne were the cherubim, winged sphinxes, with the body of a lion, the wings of an eagle, the feet of an ox and the face of a man. To the left of the throne was a table covered with cakes of bread and upon the table was the fruit from the Tree of Life. El sat enthroned between the cherubs. Seraphs flew before him, singing praises unto God. "You may take and eat from the table if you wish," El said to Daniel. But Daniel refused in blind obedience to the word of a god. Although Daniel did not know it and El did not tell him, the bread and the fruit could give immortality to the man who ate of it. Due to his blind obedience to the word of a god, mankind was denied immortality. A stool was brought for Daniel to sit upon as El spoke to him. El spoke to Daniel, "Your prayers, offerings, alms and you deeds of kindness and love have ascended into heaven as a memorial before me. Ask me of what you will and I will grant it to you." Daniel humbly answered El, "Oh God, let me have a son in my house, that he may protect me from my enemies, that he may join me when I go to the sacred places to worship the gods, that he may help me around my home, to patch my roof and wash my clothes, that he may hold me by my arm when I am old and help me when I grow weak. Let me have my own descendent, that he my erect a monument after I die, a tomb, so that my soul will not sleep forever in Sheol, but that my spirit would be awaken and freed from the earth, that my soul-my *nephesh*- may be transfigured that I may join my divine ancestors that I may become a Rephaim, the glorified and deified dead." El took a cup in his right hand and pronounced a blessing over his noble servant, "Daniel, you have taken a wife into your house. She will bear you a son and a daughter. The son you shall name Aqhat and the daughter you shall name Paghath. Your son shall be blessed. I give to him the dew of heaven and the fatness of the earth, and an abundance of grain and new wine. As for you Daniel, you are my son, this day I have begotten you. You shall rule men as king, and the son that I shall give unto you shall rule as king after you, his hands shall close your eyes in death, and he shall erect a stele for you and after you die his prayers shall transform your soul into a Rephaim. I make my covenant with you. I swear by my name, since there is no greater, that I will make of you a nation of kings and priests." Although he refused to eat of the food of the gods, El insisted that Daniel return to the world of man with a gift. He called Kothat-wa-Khasis before him. "Master builder and great craftsman, what treasure have you most recently made?" Elisha answered, "I have just finished crafting a bow for Lady Anath." As El commanded, Elisha put the bow in Daniels hands and set the arrows upon his knees." El then said, "This bow shall be the bow of Aqhat and shall be given unto him when he comes of age. El had Daniel dressed in a linen vestment and put an ephod upon him and gave unto him a Baetylus, a sacred stone with which to commune with God. And so, Elohim sent Daniel back to the world of man. He sent the Kothirath with him to bless him and his wife and to enable them to have children. And so, Daniel fathered a son and named him Aqhat. Several months thereafter, his wife again conceived and she bore him a daughter whom he named Paghath. And after the children were born, the Kothirath returned to their father El.

Aqhat and Anath

And it came to pass that Aqhat grew in wisdom, stature and strength and in favor with God and man. Daniel was a man of great wisdom and he desired to pass on his wisdom to his son Aqhat. And when Aqhat was a young man, Daniel took him and he said to him, "My son, hear the instruction of thy father, and forsake not the law of thy mother: For they shall be an ornament of grace unto thy head, and chains about thy neck. My son, if sinners entice thee, consent thou not. My son, if thou wilt receive my words, and hide my commandments within thine heart; so that thou incline thine ear unto wisdom, and apply thine heart to understanding; to know wisdom and instruction; to perceive the words of understanding; to receive the instruction of wisdom, justice, and judgment, and equity; so give subtlety to the simple, to the young man knowledge and discretion. Yea, if thou criest after knowledge and Asherah's wisdom, and liftest up thy voice for understanding; if thou seekest her as silver, and searchest for her as for hidden treasures; then shalt thou understand the fear of the ELOHIM, and find the knowledge of God. For God giveth wisdom: out of his mouth cometh knowledge and understanding. He layeth up sound wisdom for the righteous: he is a buckler to them that walk uprightly. He keepeth the paths of judgment, and preserveth the way of his holy ones. Then shalt thou understand righteousness, and judgment, and equity; yea, every good path. When wisdom entereth into thine heart, and knowledge is pleasant unto thy soul; discretion shall preserve thee, understanding shall keep thee. A wise man will hear, and will increase learning; and a man of understanding shall attain unto wise counsels: to understand a proverb, and the interpretation; the words of the wise, and their dark sayings, to deliver thee from the way of the evil man, from the man that speaketh vile things; who leave the paths of uprightness to walk in the ways of darkness. My son, forget not my law; but let thine heart keep my commandments: For length of days, and long life, and peace, shall they add to thee. Let not mercy and truth forsake thee: bind them about thy neck; write them upon the table of thine heart: So shalt thou find favour and good understanding in the sight of God and man. The fear of God is the beginning of knowledge: but fools despise wisdom and instruction."

When Aqhat became an adult, Daniel gave him the bow and he also divided the responsibilities of the kingdom with Aqhat. The king had both sacred and civil duties. Daniel took over the religious aspects of kingship. He wore the linen ephod and officiated as high priest while Aqhat took over the civil aspects of kingship. Daniel heard the difficult cases. Aqhat was also a valiant man and a great champion. He led his armies in battle and established peace by subduing his enemies. He won many great victories through his bow. He became a valiant champion. Aqhat proclaimed, "I will remove war from the earth and set love upon it. I will pour out peace unto the heart of the earth and rain down love on to the heart of the fields."

Aqhat

Paghath, the sister of Aqhat, was a woman of great virtue. She sought wool, and flax, and worked willingly with her hands. She was like the merchants' ships; she brought her food from afar. She would arise also while it was yet night, and gave food to her household, and a portion to her maidens. She considered fields, and bought them: with the fruit of her hands she planted vineyards. She girded her loins with strength, and strengthened her arms. She perceived that her merchandise was good: her lamp would not go out by night. She put her hands to the spindle, and her hands held the distaff. With compassion she stretched out her hand to the poor; yea, she reached forth her hands to the needy. She was not afraid of the snow for her household: for all her household were clothed with fine garments. She made herself coverings of tapestry; her clothing was embroidered and she wore a coat of many colours. She made fine linen, and sold it; and delivered belts unto the merchant. Strength and honour were her clothing. She opened her mouth with wisdom; and in her tongue was the law of kindness. She looked well to the ways of her household, and did not eat the bread of idleness.

The goddess Anath greatly desired the bow and she appeared to Aqhat. "Listen to me hero, if you want silver or gold, you may have all that you desire but you must give your bow and your arrows to me." Aqhat answered her, "I will give treasures unto Kothar-wa-Khasis from my own storehouse that he may forge you a new bow like this one or perhaps one better than it, but I will not give unto you the heritage of my fathers that came from El himself." Anath then said, "Then in exchange for the bow I will grant you immortality." Aqhat answered her, "Don't deceive me, goddess. You shouldn't lie to a man of action such as myself. It is evident that death is the common lot of man. I shall die and lay down with my fathers. My skull will be covered with plaster and housed in the tomb of my ancestors. My body shall decay, but my *nephesh*, my soul, shall live forever among the Rephaim. Besides, what does a woman, like yourself, need bows and arrows for? Women never hunt." Anath laughed, but her heart was filled with fury. "Listen to me he-man," she said, "Our paths will soon cross again and you will be crushed under my feet, pretty-boy." She then flew away towards El.

The goddess Anath

She barged into his tent and addressed El, "I demand vengeance upon a mortal who has mocked me." "What mortal has dishonored you?" "It was Aqhat, the son of Daniel," she answered. "You may rebuke him but you may not take his life. I forbid you to lay a finger upon him," responded El. Since she was forbidden from directly attacking Aqhat by Elohim, she decided to attack him indirectly, through her devoted worshiper Yatpan.

Anath returned to earth and found the mighty man named Yatpan. She made love to him but at a price. She demanded that he obey her commands whatever they may be without question. He pledged himself to her to be her servant. She told him, "We shall both transform into hawks. I will distract Aqhat while you knock him down and take the bow away from him."

Using her magical powers, Anath transformed herself and her slave Yatpan into the form of hawks. Anath launched her attendant Yatpan in hawk form against Aqhat to knock the breath out of him and to steal the bow back. Yatpan, in hawk form, dropped a rock upon Aqhat's head and hit him. Her plan succeeded, but Aqhat was killed by Yatpan instead of merely beaten and robbed. At the death of Aqhat, all the grass and plants began to wither and die, because his life was connected to the fertility of the earth due to the blessing pronounced upon him by El. Anath turned her rage against Yatpan, Yatpan then fled away and dropped the bow and arrows which fell into the sea. The bow was broken and lost in the sea. All was lost. As Yatpan fled away he transformed back into his human form. Anath mourned for Aqhat and for the curse that this act would bring upon the land and for the loss of the bow as well. The bloodshed brought drought to the land and mourning.

Resheph and Anath from an Egyptian monument

Anath in flight

The Vengeance of Paghath

Daniel was worshiping the Rephaim at the graves of his fathers at a place called the Bemah, or Bamah, near to the threshing fields called the Goran. A Rephaim appeared to him and told him that Aqhat had joined them in Sheol. Daniel mourned and tore his garments and put on sackcloth and ashes. His father Daniel mourned but Aqhat's sister Paghath sought vengeance. She said to herself, "I will kill my brother's killer. I shall slay him with my own hands."

Paghath, the wise younger sister of Aqhat, set off to avenge her brother's death and to restore the land which has been devastated by drought as a direct result of the murder. She journeyed to a camp with a dagger hid under her garments. Then she bathed herself, beautified herself and put on makeup and perfume. She then entered the camp and asked for the captain of the host and Yatpan appeared before her. She went into his tent and then all day and into the night she lay with him. Now when the evening was come, his servants made haste to depart, he shut his tent and dismissed his servants from his presence; and they went to their beds: for they were all weary, because they had feasted and the feast had been long. And Paghath was left alone in the tent, and Yatpan lying alone upon his bed: for he was filled with wine. So all went forth and none was left in the bedchamber, neither small nor great. Then Paghath, standing by his bed, said in her heart, "O Lord God to whom all power belongs, look at this present moment upon the works of mine hands for the exaltation of the family you have blessed. For now is the time to help thine inheritance, and to execute thine destruction of the enemies which are risen against us." Then she came to the bedpost of the bed, which was at Yatpan's head, and took down his khopesh scimitar from thence, and approached to his bed, and took hold of the hair of his head, and said, "Make me strong, O Lord God of my father Daniel, this day." And she smote twice upon his neck with all her might, and she took away his head from him. And his body tumbled down from the bed, and pulled down the canopy from the bedpost. She moved quietly and no one in the camp stirred. She then quietly and quickly went out, and went out of the camp and skirted a ravine and made good her escape. Then she secretly departed and journeyed to the sea side. There, El caused Yam the sea to give up the bow. She found it washed up in two pieces upon the beach. Then El sent Ptah in the guise of an old man and he reassembled the bow for her and gave it to her with the arrows.

Paghath

The Rephaim

In the morning the soldiers found their captain in the tent dead and they began their pursuit of Paghath. They found her at the beach holding a bow. They attacked her and with the bow she slew a thousand men. Paghath then sought her father and found him at the tombs where he had buried Aqhat near to the Goran, the threshing fields. He was still mourning Aqhat. Suddenly, the earth shook as Anath leaped down from heaven and appeared and challenged Paghath, "You have murdered my servant Yatpan. Now, give the bow to me and I will spare your life."

"No," answered Paghath, as she turned the bow upon Anath. Anath glared at her with fury, "You presume to fight me? I am the goddess of war! I have brought with me the entire army of Yatpan. You shall surely die." Paghath answered her, "I may die, but I will die fighting for the love of my brother and the honor of my family." Paghath fired an arrow at Anath. Anath caught it and crushed it to powder in her hand. "Now, I will destroy you," Anath said as the approached Paghath.

Daniel then called upon the Rephaim. "I summon you, O Rephaim! I summon you, Oh counsel of my departed fathers!" In anxiety and despair he cut himself and he was covered with his own blood.

The Rephaim appeared between Anath and Paghat and spoke to Anath, "Paghath shall not die! We call upon El for justice!" Then Daniel took out the Baethylus stone, erected it upon a column of stone, anointed it with oil and invoked El with it. Daniel cried out unto God, "El Elyon has made a covenant with us-Asherah has made a pact with us-as have all the sons of El and the great Council of all the Holy Ones with oaths of Heaven and earth of old. Be true to Thy word, O Lord."

Suddenly, Resheph and Dabir, the Guardians of El, appeared. Resheph sent out a fire that consumed the armies of Yatpan, who had become the enemies of El by seeking the harm of Daniel, a man he had proclaimed as his son. Suddenly, in his chariot surrounded by clouds, thunder and lightning, El appeared, carried by the cherubim. His voice thundered, "I am God Most High. I promised Aqhat long life and connected his life to the fertility of the land. I decree that in exchange for the bow, that Anath must restore Aqhat again to life so that the land may once again be blessed."

Anath called upon Shataqat the goddess of healing, and Eshmoun the god of healing and they restored the body of Aqhat to wholeness. Anath then poured the water of life upon Aqhat. Then El held his staff over the body of Aqhat and said to the Rephaim, "My sons, sit down upon your thrones, take your princely seats. I will work magic and I will bring relief. Death-be broken! Shataqat-be strong! Eshmoun-have power!" He then breathed into the nostrils of Aqhat the breath of life and Aqhat revived. At the resurrection of her brother, Paghath handed over the bow to Anath. El pronounced his blessing over Aqhat again and at the blessing, the plants revived. The gods then departed in to heavens and the Rephaim departed back into the deep places of the earth. And the land had peace.

And Daniel rejoiced greatly and said, "Praise be to Elohim, the God of gods. Praise his holy name with the tambourine and exalt God with timbrels. Sing unto my Lord with cymbals: sing unto him a new psalm: exalt him, and call upon his name. Praise God in his sanctuary: praise him in the firmament of his power. Praise him for his mighty acts: praise him according to his excellent greatness. Praise him with the sound of the trumpet: praise him with the psaltery and harp. Praise him with the timbrel and dance: praise him with stringed instruments and organs. Praise him upon the loud cymbals: praise him upon the high sounding cymbals. Let every thing that hath breath praise Elohim."

And Daniel lived long and was full of years. He saw his grandchildren to the fourth generation. After many years had passed, Daniel slept with his fathers. Aqhat raised a memorial to his father and performed the rites and so Daniel took his place among the Rephaim. And the descendents of Daniel ruled as kings, as the sons of El on earth. They carried the blessing of heaven and were responsible to bring order and justice to the land and to maintain God's favor.

The Baal Cycle

Part Two

LEVIATHAN

LEVIATHAN

Yam wants to rule over the other gods and be the most powerful of all

Yam, the god of the primordial chaos, the untamed and raging sea, the Lord of the Abyss, he who is called Judge Nahar, meaning "Judge River," desired to rule over all the other gods and to be the most powerful of all.

Athtar went on a journey to the edge of the sea to see the place El created as a boundary. There he encountered Yam. Yam was attempting to cross the threshold. Athtar fought against Yam but Yam could not be defeated by mighty Athtar. Yam told Athtar, "Weakling, now run away go and tell your grandfather that I shall be king and rule over all." Athtar the son of Shachar ran to Mount Leila and told El his grandfather that Yam was in rebellion.

Yam spoke contemptuously towards El, "I am Leviathan. I am the Prince of the Sea and Lord of the Rivers. I demand that you acknowledge me as your son and name me king in place of Hadad." He demanded that he be called "the favored one of God" and that God acknowledge him as his favored son. Yam threatened to destroy the sons of god and demanded tribute from them.

Ashtoreth and the Insatiable Sea

In an attempt to establish peace, Asherah went to speak with Yam and brought him gifts. Asherah went into the presence of Prince Yam. She came before Judge Nahar. She begged that He release his grip upon the gods her sons. But Mighty Yam declined her request. She offered favors to the Tyrant. But Powerful Nahar would not soften his heart. Finally, kindly Asherah, she who loves her children, offered her own body to the God of the Sea and the Lord of Rivers.

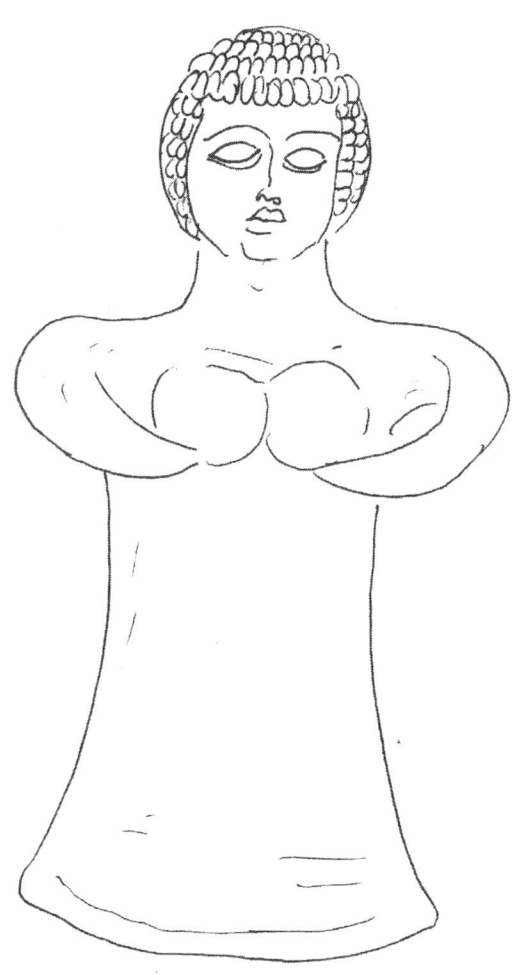

An ancient idol of Asherah

Asherah

Yam-Nahar agreed to this, and Asherah returned to the Source of the Two Rivers. She went home to the court of El. She came before the Divine Council, and spoke of her plan to the gods her children.

Baal was infuriated by her speech. He was angered at the gods who would allow such a plot. He would not consent to surrendering the Great Asherah to the tyrant Yam-Nahar. He swore to the gods that He would destroy Prince Yam. He would lay to rest the tyranny of Judge Nahar.

Yam-Nahar was made aware of the words of Baal. He sent His two messengers to the court of El. He sent his ambassadors and commanded them, "At the feet of El do not fall, do not prostrate yourselves before the Convocation of the Assembly, but declare my message! And say to the Bull, my father, El, declare this to the Convocation of the Assembly; 'The message of Yam, your lord, of your master Judge River: Give up, O gods, him whom you harbor, him whom the multitude of the gods give sanctuary! Give up Baal and His partisans, Dagon's Son, so that I may inherit His gold! I demand that Anath and Asherah be given to me as tribute.'" Yam's messengers arrived upon Mount Zaphon. They showed no honor or respect to God. Yam's ambassadors made known to the Divine Assembly his demands. They were to offer up to him Asherah, Ashtoreth, and Anath and Baal Haddad was to be banished from the counsel of the sons of God. The gods lowered their heads to their knees. Haddad rebuked them for their lack of courage as they sat upon their princely seats.

Prince Baal was infuriated. He took out his khopesh sickle-sword to smite the ambassadors for their insolence. But, Anath seized His right hand and Ashtoreth seized His left hand: "How canst thou smite the messengers of Yam? The emissaries of Judge Nahar? They have merely brought the words of Yam-Nahar their Lord and Master." But Prince Baal was enraged. He spared the lives of the messengers; he sent them back to their master after giving them a good beating. He instructed them to give his information: "Baal will not bow down to Prince Yam. He will not be the slave of Judge Nahar. He declares once more that he shall slay the tyrant lord of the gods." But the Divine Assembly decided to offer up Anath and Ashtoreth to Yam in the hopes that this offering would placate Yam. They delivered this message to Yam and when he heard that Anath and Ashtoreth were his to take he smiled and was glad.

Asherah willingly surrendered herself to Yam. She took with her only her pet serpent Nehushtan and a golden bowl as a gift for Yam. Nehushtan was her protector and a serpent who could not be charmed. Asherah stood upon the shore. Yam caused the stone upon which she stood to break off and float out into the sea. With her floating upon the waters, she was in his power, as he was the master of the seas. He climbed out upon the rock that he might ravish her. Then he grasped and squeezed her arm. Yam was dismayed when he saw that the flesh he had grasped was turning into a branch of a tree. Asherah then assumed her tree-form and took the shape of an olive tree. Then, Asherah caused herself to burst in the flames. While the tree burned, it was not consumed by the flame. Nehushtan was entwined around the trunk of the tree and around the branches. The golden bowl also rested upon its base. El had sent an eagle to watch over Asherah. He rested upon the branches. The flame did no harm to the serpent, nor to the eagle, nor to the bowl. But the fire would burn the tentacles and claws of Yam whenever he tried to touch Lady Asherah.

Asherah surrenders herself to Yam the Leviathan

The Ambrosian Stone

Yam was angered and dismayed and caused the Island to float off into the distant waters. Though he was unable to rape Asherah, he comforted himself knowing that Anath and Ashtoreth would soon be within his power and that he could unleash his fury and frustration upon them.

And the servants of Yam traveled to the temple of Anath to take her captive. Anath had her attendants beautify her. She had herself washed anointed with perfumes and adorned herself. She prepared herself by anointing herself with henna and ambergris, and dressing in gold saffron and multi-colored clothing, both of expensive, and royal, colors. She had her eyes lined with kohl. She had intricate patterns dyed on her hands and feet with henna. She took her seat at her house and waited for the soldiers of Yam to arrive. When they arrived, they demanded that she come with them and present herself to Yam. "Surely I will go with you-if one of you can make me." She then undressed before them, saying, "But for now, I have chosen a more suitable attire, let me now change my garments." Once she was undressed, she suddenly hurled chairs at the troops, hurled tables at the soldiers, footstools at the heroes of Yam. She slew them. She chopped off their heads and made them into a necklace. She chopped off their arms and made them into a skirt. She clothed herself with their heads and arms. She waded waist-deep through their gore and innards. And yet her lust for blood was not sated. She left her house and found a regiment of the soldiers of Yam and slew them all. Wild and ferocious as a warrior in battle, the furious Anath smote her enemies. She waded knee-deep in their blood and entrails, striking off heads. Heads rolled under her like balls. Hands flew around her like locusts. She bound the heads upon her torso and the hands upon her sash. Driving at them with her arrows from the bow of Aqhat filled her heart with joy. And after she had made a great slaughter she bathed her feet in the blood of her enemies, then she was satisfied and returned to her home and rested.

One soldier survived and returned and told Yam that Anath had singlehandedly destroyed one of his armies. And Yam was in dismay and was greatly angered. He demanded that this time, the gods deliver Ashtoreth up to him, bring her to him in chains, unarmed and striped of her enchanted armor, at an appointed time and chain her upon a rock at the sea side so that he may take her and have his way with her. The sons of God agreed to her request. El called Baal Haddad in private. He told him, "You must fight against Yam for my glory. Go to Kothar-wa-Khasis that he may provide you with weapons so that you may use them when you fight against Yam in order to save your sister Ashtoreth from his evil devices. Then you must seek for my wife upon the seas, once you have mastered them, and bring Lady Asherah back to me."

Anath destroys an army belonging to Yam

Baal the Conqueror opposes Yam and slays him

Baal Hadad traveled to the land of Egypt, to a city called Noph and there he sought out Ptah according to the word of El that Ptah might provide him with magical weapons. Noph was called by the Egyptians *Men-nefer* (meaning "enduring and beautiful"), Men-nefer was pronounced as "Memphis" by the Greeks. He arrived at the port of the city, which was called *Peru-nefer*, in the Egyptian language. The port harboured a high density of workshops, factories, and warehouses that distributed food and merchandise throughout the ancient kingdom of Egypt. He entered the house of Ptah which was called *Hut-ka-Ptah* (meaning "Enclosure of the ka, meaning soul, of Ptah"), the name of this temple, rendered in Greek as *Ai-gy-ptos,* and the Greek named all of the land of Egypt after this great house. Ptah, who is called Kothar-wa-Khasis, he who is skillful and wise, the holy craftsman of the gods, created weapons for Lord Haddad. And Kothar-wa-Khasis declared: "I proclaim to thee, O Prince Baal, unto you I declare, O Rider of Clouds- 'Lo, thine enemies, O Baal, Lo, thine enemies wilt thou smite lo, thou shalt vanquish thy foes. Thou wilt take thine eternal kingdom; thine everlasting sovereignty! O Storm-rider, thy dominion shall last forever and ever!'"

Kothar brought down two weapons and proclaimed their names. The first, a lightning bolt spear, he named Yagrush saying "Thy name, even thine, is Yagrush! The Expeller! Yagrush, expel Yam! Drive Yam from His throne. Drive Nahar from the seat of His sovereignty! Thou shalt swoop from the hands of Baal like an eagle from His fingers! Strike the shoulders of Prince Yam betwixt the hands of Judge Nahar!" Kothar then brought down a second weapon, a mace, and proclaims its name, Aymur the Chaser. Elisha said, "Thy Name, even thine, is Aymur! Aymur, chase Yam, from His throne! Nahar from His seat of His sovereignty! Thou shalt swoop from the hands of Baal like an eagle from His fingers! Strike the head of Prince Yam between the eyes of Judge Nahar! Let Yam sink! You, O Haddad, will take your eternal kingship, your dominion will last forever and ever."

Zeus hurling his thunderbolts-an image likely originally derived from Baal Haddad

Baal Haddad wielding Yagrush and Aymur from an ancient artifact

At the appointed time, Ashtoreth was chained to a rock at an outcropping of at the edge of the sea at Joppa. And so Yam arose from the waters. From where she was chained upon a rock on the seashore she looked and behold, she saw a beast, rising from out of the sea. It had seven heads and horns upon its heads and wore crowns upon its horns. It was Yam the Leviathan. Ashtoreth screamed in terror at the sight of his horrific appearance. Yam reached out to grab Ashtoreth with his talons. Suddenly, Baal Hadad appeared riding upon the clouds of the sky. He smote the claw of Yam with his lightning bolt. Anath then appeared carrying her sword. With it she broke the chains that bound Ashtoreth and implored her to help them in the fight against the Leviathan. But, once she was released Ashtoreth fled away seized with terror, leaving Hadad and Anath to fight Yam alone. Anath shouted out to Hadad, "I will fight with you till death if need be." Haddad smote off one of the heads of Yam but another grew back in its place. Haddad hurled his bolt of lightning. The lightning flashed, the thunder rumbled, the earth trembled and the waters churned.

Anath stamped her foot and the earth shook. Anath sent arrows into the heart of Yam firing them with the bow of Aqhat. And the weapons sprang from the hand of Baal, like a raptor from between his fingers. It struck the skull of Prince Yam, it hit between the eyes of Judge Nahar. Yam collapsed, he fell to the earth. Haddad crushed the skulls of Yam, one by one. Yam's joints quivered and his spine shook. Then, thus spoke Yam, "Lo, I am good as dead. Surely now Baal reigns as king!" Haddad and Anath smote the seven headed dragon Leviathan, the Twisting Serpent. Yam finally fell due to the wounds inflicted upon him by Baal and Anath. Thereupon Baal Haddad drug out Yam from the waters and rent him to pieces. He made an end of Judge Nahar. Baal lifted up his death body and carried it to land. There he laid it out so that the birds of the air and the wild beast of the field could feast upon it.

Seeing that Baal had gotten the best of Yam, Ashtoreth returned and shouted praises to Baal's name. With her was Ariel, the lion of god, who protected her. (Ariel, the Lion of El, is also called Arioch, meaning, "the Fierce Lion.") Ashtoreth shouted, "Hail, Baal the Conqueror! Hail to the rider on the clouds! Praises be to the Storm-rider! For Prince Sea is our captive and we have imprisoned Judge River." At his victory the sons of God declared, "Our King is Baal the Conqueror." Baal was given the name Aliyan, meaning the Victorious. His name Haddad means "the Thunderer." He was also called the cloud rider-"rakiba arapati" and Majesty, the Lord of Earth-"Zubulu baalu arsi."

An ancient idol of Anath the goddess of War

Anath the goddess of war

Ashtoreth with Ariel

An ancient Greco-Syrian coin bearing the image of Atargatis riding upon a lion. Atargatis may have had her origins in Ashtoreth.

Baal Haddad

Baal Haddad had committed himself to rescuing Lady Asherah from the Sea. So, he sat and thought about how he could accomplish his. He devised a plan and committed himself to a course of action. He went to Ptah and requested that he would design and build him a boat. He went to the region of Tyre and Sidon and he called the men to him. He promised great riches to the men who would join him on a sea quest. Many men did volunteer and he set them to work building a bireme. This was a galley ship with two rows of oars on each side. It employed 120 rowers. Ptah supervised the men as they labored building the boat. When the ship was completed Ptah had eyes painted on either side of the prow as a magical sign of divine protection. The eyes were the Wadjet, the sacred eye symbol from Egypt, his country. There the Wadjet was painted on both boats and funerary equipment, as a protection against all manner of evils. The Wadjet is a symbol of protection, royal power and good health. Ancient Egyptian and Near Eastern sailors would frequently paint the symbol on the bow of their vessel to ensure safe sea travel. To this day Mediterranean boats still have these eyes painted on, to guard against losing their way and as a guarantee against getting lost or running into something. (Later, the magical Wadjet eye came to be acquired by Horus and so it became also known as the Eye of Horus, whose tale is told in the Ennead.) Ptah imbued the ship with a spirit. He erected a shrine upon the ship wherewith to worship El and he named the ship Hannibal, meaning, "the Grace of Baal," saying that the ship would sail with the grace of Baal. Baal Haddad found a man who was industrious and wise and he made him his lieutenant. His name was Sid Addir. Sid was a great hunter and a mighty warrior. He was pleased with his work and so he adopted him as his own son. Baal Haddad also brought along his dog, a saluki, for the journey. They set sail and had many adventures as they sailed across the Great Sea. The dolphins followed the bireme during the entire journey.

When the ship stopped at Cyprus, Sid found a stowaway who had hidden in the hull. He brought her before Lord Haddad. Baal asked her who she was and why she had stowed away in his ship. She was thought to be a worthless woman. Lord Haddad reproved her saying, "There is no room for a shameful, degrading and wanton woman upon this vessel." She protested and claimed to be a woman of virtue. She said that her name was Elisshat. She was called Alyssa. She was the eighteen year old daughter of King Mattan. King Mattan had decided that she and her brother Ben-Mattan, would rule jointly after his death. She was married to the high priest Zakarbaal, her uncle, three years ago. Zakarbaal was kind and loving to her. Recently, her father died. After he was buried, Ben-Mattan murdered Zakarbaal and threatened to execute Alyssa as well, unless she surrendered the Ephod of Zakarbaal, which he had sought, to him. Ben-Mattan had no intention of sharing his rule with anyone, despite his father's wishes. Alyssa was able to escape and to secretly retrieve the ephod, which she wore hidden under her garments. (The Ephod is a priestly vestment that contained the jewel embedded pectoral patterned after the one worn by Adam in the Garden of Eden. The Ephod is also an oracle.) The reason she had stowed away was to save her own life and to keep the Ephod of Zakarbaal from falling into Ben-Mattan's hands. Haddad spoke to her and was impressed with her wisdom, grace and beauty. He promised to protect her from harm. Alyssa offered to consult the Ephod to use it to find the way to Asherah. She said, "We can use the Ephod to divine the way to Asherah." (The Ephod would give a yes or no answer to the question posed to it.) Upon the island of Cyrus they also found twelve judges who had fled from the court of Ben-Mattan, whom they described as a tyrant and a villain. Haddad invited them to join him on his quest and they agreed to accompany them. Haddad promised to find a new land in which they would dwell.

Zakarbaal the Priest

They sailed across the Great Sea for many days. In the distant land of Tarshish, Haddad built a sanctuary for the gods and called it Cadiz. He dedicated Cadiz to his parents, Baal Hammom and Tanit, and also to Lady Asherah, whom he still sought. Then Haddad and his men continued their journey into the distant ocean.

They sailed towards the north. There a party went ashore to procure some supplies from the local peoples. They encountered a tall people with golden hair and blue eyes. They were Germans. The men of Tyre and Sidon said, "We are unto them like unto grasshopper and so we seem so unto them." They were of such a great stature that to them the Phoenicians seemed to be dwarves. For food and garments, the Phoenicians traded jewelry with the Germans. The Germans were amazed at the craftsmanship and asked many questions. The Phoenicians told the Germans of the turquoise that they had mined in the Sinai. The Germans were amazed and took the Phoenicians to be of a supernatural race and they called them the Dark Elves, because most of the Phoenicians had black hair and much darker complexions than the Germans. The Germans were friendly towards the Phoenicians and made a covenant of friendship with them.

As they continued north, they saw mountains of ice floating in the ocean. After many days in the deep, Sid called for Baal Haddad. "I see a small island upon which there looks to be a bush that is burning but is not consumed. Let us go and see this strange sight!" They went ashore to the island and saw that it was floating. When Baal Haddad approached the burning tree, he at once recognized it as Lady Asherah. Alyssa consulted the Ephod and it confirmed that the burning tree was indeed Asherah. Haddad then immediately commanded the men to tie ropes around the floating island in order to tow it with the boat. Baal Haddad, as the Lord of the Storm-wind, caused a breeze to blow upon the ship to give it fair winds.

On their return journey, they arrived at the north coast of Africa and made port. There they were greeted by a Berber chieftan named Hairbash who welcomed them to his territory. Alyssa saw the land and was pleased with it. She offered to purchase land from Hairbash. He agreed to sell land to them, but only as much as could be covered by an ox hide. The judges cut the hide out into very thin strips and were thus able to mark out a larger and more pleasing area. Hairbash was displeased but bound by his word. Alyssa named the city she founded Qart-Haddashat, or Carthage, meaning the New City. Haddad crowned her queen and gave her the throne name of Dido. (Dido means "the traveler." She was given this name due to her travels.) The judges married priestesses who had accompanied them in the ship and thus began settling the new colony. The city immediately became prosperous. Many came there to settle and to trade. Haddad and his companions blessed Queen Dido and then departed to continue on to their destination. Queen Dido's reign was long and just. She established a constitutional republic. And it came to pass, that after many years, she sought love but was spurned by her lover and died of a broken heart without producing an heir. However, the democratic system she established endured for centuries until it was destroyed by a band of savage and wicked men from the north who were traitors and villains.

Alyssa as Queen Dido

The company of Haddad neared home. They brought the stone, towing it to the coast of Phoenicia, from whence they had began their journey, and anchored it there. Once there, Lord Haddad approached the tree. Baal Haddad reached through the flame, which did not harm him, and took the eagle. He gave it to the priests of the people and they sacrificed it to El. The spirit of the eagle immediately returned to El and notified him that Asherah had returned. When the blood from the eagle dripped upon the rock it immediately became rooted to the bottom of the sea and grew into a large island. At that Asherah transformed herself into her human form once again. She gave the golden bowl to the priests and commanded that they would keep it as a sacred relic in a sanctuary. The men began building a temple and a city upon the rock. The people named Asherah the Belat, or the Lady, of the city and called Baal Haddad, Melqart, meaning "King of the City" and they named the island-city Tyre, meaning "rock," after the rock of Asherah. They also called Asherah *Rabbatu Atiratu Yammi*-the Lady Goddess of the Sea. Asherah left Tyre to return to the Mountain of El. The city of Tyre was built upon this island which had floated across the sea. The floating stone that became Tyre was later called "the Ambrosian Stone." Seated on the throne of Tyre, Haddad commanded, "Bring before me the tyrant Ben-Mattan." He was brought before Haddad. Haddad commanded his men to execute him in his sight and the men obeyed his command.

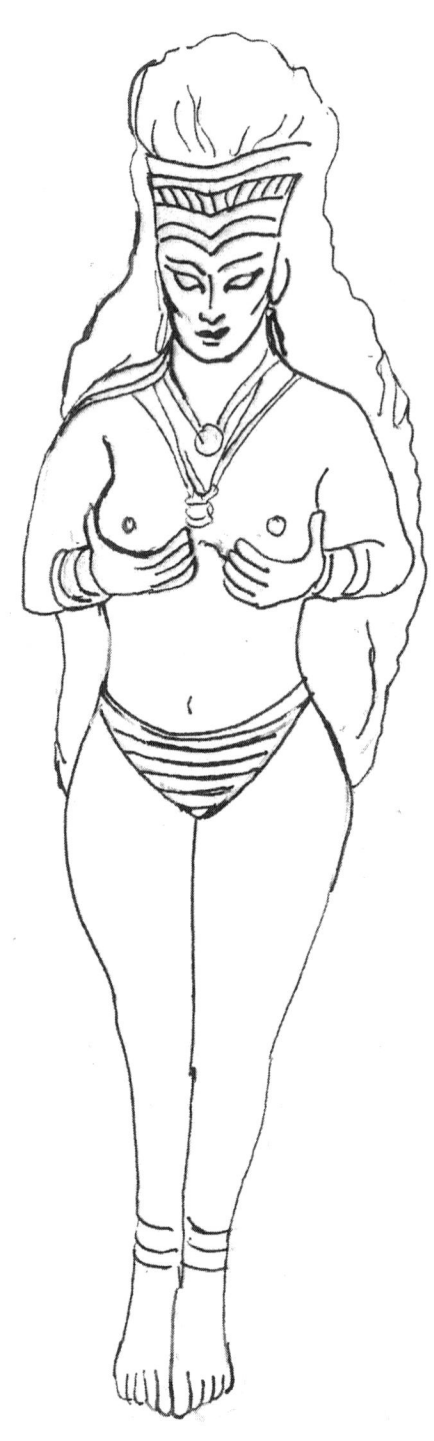

An ancient idol of Asherah

Baal walked along the beach and thought about what sort of reward he should give the men of Tyre. While he was walking along the beach his dog, who was accompanying him, devoured a murex snail and gained a beautiful purple color around its mouth. Seeing this, Haddad gathered many murex shells, extracted the dye from them, and dyed the first garment of the colour later called Tyrian purple. He taught the men of Tyre to do the same and the people of Tyre became very wealthy by making and trading the purple garments.

Baal Hadad with Anath at his side journeyed across the face of the earth and did mighty exploits. They crushed the river demon, Rabbim. They annihilated the fire god and battled the dark god Baal Zebub, the Lord of Flies. Haddad then set out to pacify the towns of the marauders. One of their recalcitrant chieftans styled himself King Pabil. Haddad sent his servant Keret against him. He gave him these orders, "Don't shoot arrows into his city nor sling-stones into his fortress. Instead march around the city cheering and blowing the trumpets. Do this until the evening of the seventh day." On the evening of the seventh day, King Pabil surrendered to Keret. He was brought before Haddad and was forced to lay prostrate at his feet. Haddad put his foot upon King Pabil's neck but spared his life. Haddad and Anath conquered seventy-seven cities and established peace upon the earth. They won possession of much silver and gold. Baal then sat down upon his throne of glory. To show him honor at his coronation, Anath and Ashtoreth assumed the form of cherubim and sat one at his right and the other at his left on each side of his throne.

Ashtoreth in the form of a Cherub (taken from an image from Ancient Egypt)

Anath, Baal Haddad and Ashtoreth

El becomes drunk

Soon after the return of Haddad and Anath, the gods celebrated with a great feast. Baal served the gods and goddesses a thousand jugs of wine. He said to them, "It is I who feed gods and men." El entertained himself with the goddess Pidray, the plump damsel, the maid of light, and the goddesses Talia, the maid of rain, and the earth-maiden Arsay, the maid of floods and dallied with them. He became so drunk that he fell upon the ground upon his face and wallowed in his own vomit. Meth looked upon him and despised him in his heart and began plotting in his mind to seize the throne. He secretly went to El while he was in his drunken stupor and took from off of his neck the Tablets of Destiny and hid them within his own garments. He took from El the Tablets of Destinies, which were not rightfully his, and hid them on his person. He did this secretly and no one saw him do this. Then the kindly Anath and Ashtoreth saw their father sprawled out upon the floor and laying in his own vomit, they helped him up and carried him to his throne and helped him sit down. Then they gave him medicine so that he would recover from his drunkenness and held it up to his lips so that he would drink of it. After he took the medicine, they took him to his chamber, the removed the ornaments he wore and his garments, the then goddesses helped him to bed, they warmed his body with theirs and comforted him there.

Lady Isis appears before Melqart and Queen Ashtoreth

And it came to pass one day that an ornate chest which was gilded and embedded with many jewels washed up upon the shore near the city of Gebel. It became entangled in the branches of a tamarisk tree. Asherah caused the tree to totally envelope the chest. Soon this tree, which was a manifestation of the goddess Asherah, became famous throughout all the land. Presently King Melqart heard of it, and he and his wife, Queen Ashtoreth, came to the seashore to gaze at the tree. King Melqart gave orders that the tree should be cut down and fashioned into a great pillar in the Temple of El, his father. This was done, and all wondered at its beauty and the fragrance it emitted.

After having wandered from Egypt throughout the land of Canaan searching for the chest which held the body of her murdered husband Osiris, Isis, the queen of Egypt, came to Byblos and sat down by the seashore. Presently the maidens who attended on Queen Ashtoreth came down to bathe at that place; and when they returned out of the water Isis befriended them and taught them how to plait their hair in the Egyptian style - which had never been done before. When they went up to the Temple of El, where Ashtoreth and Haddad were dwelling, a strange and wonderful perfume seemed to cling to them; and Queen Ashtoreth marveled at it, and at their braided hair, and asked them how it came to be so. The maidens told her of the wonderful woman who sat by the seashore, and Queen Astarte sent for Isis, and asked her to serve in the temple compound and tend the children there. Isis blessed the children of the temple and healed all those who were sick in the city of their ailments. Ashtoreth did not know that the strange woman who was wandering alone at Gebel was the greatest of all the goddesses of Egypt. But later when Isis appeared before Melqart and Ashtoreth at court of El's Temple, Melqart recognized her as a goddess. Then Melqart and Astoreth offered her gifts of all the richest treasures in Byblos, but Isis asked only for the great tamarisk pillar which held up the roof of the temple, and for what it contained. When it was given to her, she caused it to be opened and took out from within it the chest that was built by Seth the Usurper as a coffin for Osiris. When the chest which had become the coffin of Osiris was given to her, Isis flung herself down on it with a terrible a cry of sorrow. She had cracked open the Sacred Asherah Pole and healed it after she had released her beloved from within and restored the Asherah Pole whole. She took the golden chest but the pillar she gave back to Melqart and Astoreth; and it remained the most sacred object in Byblos, because it had once held the body of a god and since it was holy to Asherah. It was erected as the Asherah pole, or xoanon, in the Temple of God. (This Asherah pole was an incarnation of Lady Asherah. She held Osiris within her and he was born of Lady Asherah and Isis served as midwife when she opened up the Asherah pole containing Osiris and delivered him from within her. When the chest had washed ashore it came into Asherah's embrace and she wrapped her arms around it and hid it within herself to protect it for its rightful owner.) Isis worshiped El and Asherah. Then she stated that she would was going to take Osiris to Egypt to awaken him. All the people mourned when they heard that the Lady Isis would be departing from them. Isis at length caused the chest to be placed on a boat which King Melqart provided for her, and set out for Egypt and there Osiris was restored to life. The rest of the acts of Isis, from first to last, are they not written in the Book of the Great Ennead?

Isis

The coffin of Osiris engulfed within a Tamarisk tree

Baal-Haddad, with the help of Anath and Asherah, persuades El to allow him a palace

El erected his holy tabernacle at Mount Zephon to dwell there for a while. Baal requested that he be allowed to build himself a palace upon Mount Zephon. He requested this from his father El. El hesitated to grant Baal's request. Haddad was the son of Tanith and not the son of Asherah. Therefore, it was necessary for him to first seek permission from Lady Asherah to build his palace upon Mount Zaphon and build his throne at the place where the seventy sons of Asherah would meet. He asked his mother Tanith if she would request audience for him with her mother Asherah. She did so and Asherah consented.

An Egyptian depiction of the goddess Qudshu-believed to be Asherah or Ashtoreth

Then Lord Haddad approached Lady Asherah of the Sea, the Mother Goddess and the Queen of Heaven, (*Malkath haShamayim*). As he approached her presence, she spoke, saying, "El possessed me in the beginning of his way, before his works of old. I was set up from everlasting, from the beginning, before ever the earth was. When there were no depths, I was brought forth; when there were no fountains abounding with water. Before the mountains were settled, before the hills was I brought forth: While as yet he had not made the earth, nor the fields, nor the highest part of the dust of the world. When he prepared the heavens, I was there: when he set a measurement upon the face of the depth: When he established the clouds above: when he strengthened the fountains of the deep: When he gave to the sea his decree, that the waters should not pass his commandment: when he appointed the foundations of the earth: Then I was by him, as one brought up with him: and I was daily his delight, rejoicing always before him; rejoicing in the habitable part of his earth; and my delights were with the sons of men. Now therefore hearken unto me, O child: for blessed are they that keep my ways. Heed instruction, and be wise, and refuse it not. Blessed is he that heareth me, watching daily at my gates, waiting at the posts of my doors. I am a *Tree of Life* to those who take hold of me; those who hold me fast will be blessed. For whoso findeth me findeth life, and shall obtain favour of the El. But he that sinneth against me wrongeth his own soul: all they that hate me love death."

Lord Haddad offered her gifts and bowed down low before her and showed her great honor. He requested her permission that a house be built for him like the houses built for her sons. She received his gifts and granted him her approval that a house be built for him. Haddad then asked his sister Anath to approach El with a request that he be granted permission to build his palace upon Mount Zaphon.

El stands outside of his Tabernacle

Anath stamped her foot and the earth shook. She soared into the heavens. She went straight to El. She journeyed to the source of the two rivers, the abode of El. El had since returned to his holy mountain. She barged into El's royal compound. She burst into the tent of the Great King El, the father of time. She then addressed El, "How can you rejoice with your sons and celebrate with your daughters? How is it that those about you are happy? Grant me what I desire, or so help me, I will smash your skull open and pour out your brains. I will cut you open and spill out your innards. Then I will force feed you your own intestines." El quietly chuckled and then after a pause he spoke, "Oh my daughter, you are a great warrior. No one can surpass your ferocity. What is it that you would have me to do for you?" She answered, ""Lo there is no house unto Baal like the gods. Not a court like the sons of Asherah. Asherah has given her approval for Haddad's wish to build a house. Let a house be built for Haddad." Lady Asherah of the Sea then opened El's tent and entered the shrine of the Father of Time. She bowed down before El, the Ancient of Days, in adoration. She prostrated herself before him and worshiped him. As soon as he saw her, El opened his mouth and laughed. His fingers danced with excitement, He raised his voice and shouted., "Why has Lady Asherah of the Sea arrived? Why has the mother of the gods come? Are you hungry or thirsty? Have something to eat or drink. Eat some food from the table. Drink some wine from the goblet. Or does the passion of El the king excite you? Does the love of the Bull arouse you?" And she answered, "Your decree is wise, O God and your wisdom is eternal. Let a temple be built for Baal. A house in honor of Lord Haddad." And the God of Mercy replied: "Am I to act as a lackey of Asherah? Am I to act like the holder of a trowel? And yet, a house shall be built for Baal like the gods. Yea, a court like the sons of Asherah. Tell Baal, "Call a caravan into your house. The mountains will bring you silver and the hills in abundance of gold. Let the camels bring you jewels to adorn the house that you shall build." Anath then thanked her father and blessed and praised his name. Then she leaped up and flew to Baal and cried out to him, "Know this, O Baal! Thy news I bring! A house shall be built for thee as for thy brothers, even a court as for thy kin! The mountains will bring thee much silver. The hills, the choicest of gold; the mines will bring thee precious stones, and build a house of silver and gold. A house of lapis gems!"

Lord Haddad

Baal-Hadad commissions Kothar-wa-Khasis to build him a palace.

A palace was build for Baal upon Mount Zaphon. It was made with cedar wood and precious metals were used for bricks. Baal sent for greedy Mammon, the god of gold, silver, treasures and wealth, and demanded tribute from him from Mammon's *Genizah*, his treasure-house hidden deep in the mines, to take from it treasures with which he could build his palace. And Mammon gave to Haddad the material with which to build his house. Kothar-wa-Khasis took the materials and with them he built the Temple of Baal. Two columns were erected at the front of the House of the Lord, the Temple of Baal Haddad. One pillar was pure gold and the other pillar was emerald. The tops of the columns were decorated with pomegranates, the emblem of Baal, who is also known as Lord Rimmon. A Sea of Brass was erected before the House of Baal as a memorial to commemorate his victory over Yam.

A palace was built for Ba'al Hadad with cedars from Mount Lebanon and Sirion and also from silver and from gold. In his new palace Ba'al hosted a great feast for the other gods. Haddad made preparations within his palace for his feast. He slaughtered oxen, he killed sheep, bulls, fatling rams, yearling calves; he strangled lambs and kids. He invited his brothers to his feast and his cousins within his palace; he invited Asherah's seventy sons. He gave the gods lambs and ewes, oxen and cows. He gave the gods seats, thrones and he gave the gods and goddesses jars of wine until the gods has eaten and drunk their full.

Baal initially refused to have a window built in his Temple. But, when urged by Kothar-wa-Khasis, Ba'al, somewhat reluctantly, opened a window in his palace. He then opened the window and sent forth thunder and lightning.

Anat played the lyre and sang songs of affection to Baal, her beloved. To celebrate his victory over Yam and the building of his house, Baal took his sisters, the goddesses, to the roof of his house, and there he made love to them. So they pitched a tent for Haddad upon the roof, and he slept with the goddesses in the sight of all. And Baal made love to Pidray, the maid of light, to Talia, the maid of rain and Arsay, the earth-maiden. Ashtoreth conceived and gave birth to the three daughters of Baal. The first daughter she named Jemimah, meaning "little dove," the second Keziah, meaning "Cinnamon," and the third Keren-Happuch, meaning "bottle of make-up (or Mascara)." And Anath conceived and gave birth to a child she named Adonai, or Adonis, meaning the Lord. But Baal named him *Dumuzi*, "the faithful and true son," but in the Aramaic language this name was pronounced Tammuz. Anath also had a daughter who was born with Tammuz as his twin sister and she gave her the name Geshtinana. And Tammuz and Geshtinana loved each other very deeply. Tammuz grew to be strong and handsome. Baal named Tammuz as the king of the shepherds and blessed his pastures that they may be ever green. Baal named Geshtinana the "heavenly grape-vine" and made her the goddess of the vineyards.

Qedem and Erebu

One of the servants of Thoth was a scribe named Zerah. He was called Qedem and was called Cadmus by the barbarians. Zerah was a prince of Tyre. He was the son of King Agenor of Tyre. King Agenor's wife, Queen Telephassa, bore him twins; a boy and a girl. He named the boy Zerah, sunrise and also called him Qedem, the east, from whence the sun rises, and named his daughter Erebu, which meant "to go down, to set," in reference to the Sun. Thus the names of his children meant Sunrise and Sunset or East and West. When he was a young man, Qedem went to Egypt to study there and to gain wisdom from the wise men of Egypt and from the god Thoth. When he returned to his homeland, Qedem created the alphabet having derived the letters from the sacred writing of the Egyptians that he had learned from Thoth. His sister was also very wise and Qedem taught her his alphabet. Erebu was a priestess who was devoted to the worship of El and to the goddess Hathor. (The cow-goddess Hathor was a goddess of sexual pleasure and motherhood. The story of Hathor is told in the Ennead of Egypt.) And Erebu was comely and very pleasant to look upon. Many men across the world came to Tyre to hear the wisdom of Qedem and to marvel at his sister's beauty. The stories of his wisdom and his sister's beauty spread across the earth. Qedem left the region of Tyre to teach the men of Sidon his alphabet. After many days had past, brigands from the west attacked Tyre, the plundered the city and abducted Erebu and carried her away in a ship to a distant land to the west. She was repeatedly raped by the men who had captured her. Several days after the raid and the kidnapping of his sister, Qedem returned to the region of Tyre from Sidon. When he learned of her abduction, he tore his garments. Then Qedem immediately went out in pursuit of his sister's captors. While pursuing them, he established Phoenician colonies and trading posts in the west. Erebu was far more wise and clever than her captors and she enslaved them and came to rule over them. Two sons were products of the gang rape she was subjected to. She named her sons Rhadamanth and Zarpedon. She took one of her captors that she had taken captive and made him her puppet king and called him King Asterion. In the tongue of the barbarians she was called "Europa" and she gave her name to the kingdom and the land that she ruled. Queen Europa taught her subjects to worship the Bull El. She also taught civilization to the savages and instructed them in reading and writing and she introduced to them the alphabet that her brother Qedem had invented. She had a Golden Calf created as a symbol of El and she instructed the people to worship it. She sat upon the Golden Calf and led the people in worship of El. Often they would dance around the Golden Calf and strip naked and engage in love-making around the Calf. After many years of searching, Qedem found Erebu. He met her sons, Rhadamanth and Zarpedon who had by then grown and were mighty men and who both served as Shophets, or judges, over the people. Qedem asked Erebu to return with him Phoenicia but she refused and said that Europe was now her home. Qedem slept with his sister and left the following day to return to Phoenicia. And yet he also never returned. He died at Thebes, a city that he had founded, and which was originally named Cadmeia in his honor. And Erebu had conceived and bore another son and named him Minos. After many years, Erebu died and her son Minos, since he was of pure Tyrian blood, being the son of Cadmus and Europa, inherited her throne. And in his wayward zeal for El he offered illicit sacrifices. At times he would offer up children as an offering to the Bull El, a sacrifice that El did not request nor desire. The gods were pleased with the way that Rhadamanth and Zarpedon administered justice and so when they died, they were made the judges of the dead. All men and women who die stand before Rhadamanth and Zarpedon, who judge them according to their works. In Sheol the evil are tormented and the just are comforted.

Europa teaches her people to worship the Bull El-in the form of a golden calf

The Epic of Baal

Part Three

BEHEMOTH

BEHEMOTH

King of the gods and ruler of the world seeks to subjugate Mot

Baal would often sit in his palace deep in thought. While sitting in his palace Lord Haddad asked himself whether anyone would dare to resist his power. He decided to hold a banquet at which all would acknowledge the rule of Baal Haddad. He sent two messengers to Meth, who is Death personified, and invited him to a feast and there to acknowledge his sovereignty. Baal's servants Gupin-wa-Ugar and Qodesh-wa-Amrur delivered the message of their master to Death. Meth refused to come and replied that he, like a lion in the desert, hungers constantly for human flesh and blood. He said, "As the deer pants for the water-brook, my desire is for slaughter. My desire is to kill and to pile up the slain into great heaps. I will crush you in my jaws like a lion crushes a goat kid." Meth claimed that by inviting him to a meal of bread and wine, Lord Haddad has offended him. Meth then threatened to cause the heavens to wilt and collapse, thus breaking Baal into pieces. Meth then threatened to eat him piece by piece. Baal demanded that Meth appear before his throne. Meth did come and spoke to Haddad contemptuously. To the surprise of Baal he pulled out the Tablets of Destiny. Meth spoke, "I am the possessor of the Tablets of Destiny and am thus the Lord of Fate. I decree that you shall submit yourself to me. By killing Yam you have created unbalance. By destroying Sea you have upset the order of the cosmos and have disrupted the balance of nature. For that you shall surely die. My mouth is like an open grave and it shall consume you." Meth had secretly held the Tablets of Destiny and was biding his time, but now he had decided to act. Meth destined Baal Haddad to journey to Mount Kankaniya in the Netherworld and there to descend into the throat of Death and enter the mouth of Hell at the gates of Death.

Meth had stolen the Tablets of Destiny

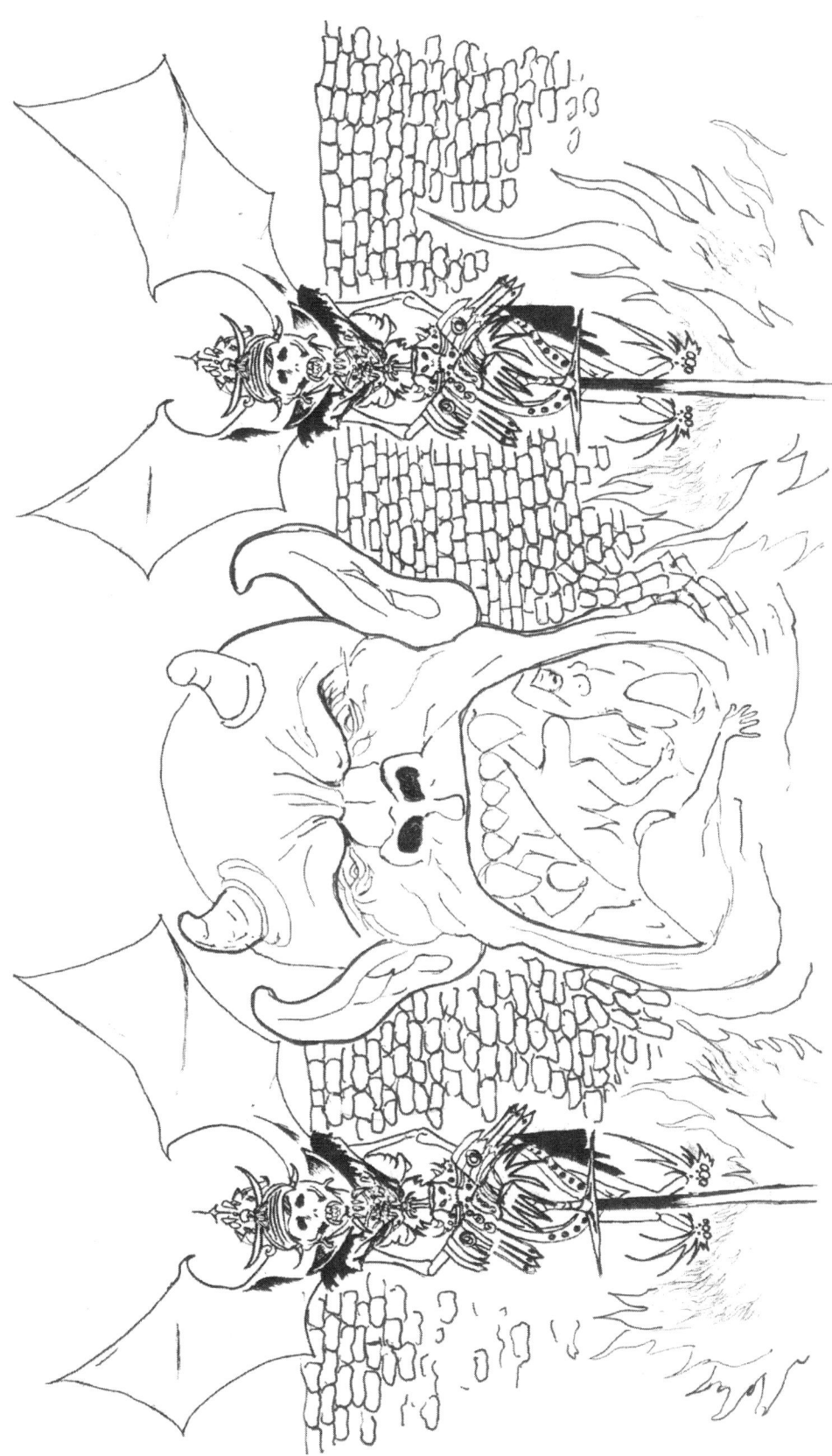

The Gates of Death

Mot kills Baal-Hadad

Meth demanded that Lord Haddad come into the realm of Sheol and surrender to him. As Meth now controlled his destiny, Baal was forced to consent to his demand. Shamash advised Baal to request a week long reprieve from Meth. This request was granted. For those seven days and seven nights he engaged in love-making with the heifer, his sister, Anath. When their time together had expired, Baal told Anath that because Meth now possessed the Tablets of Destiny he had to go and surrender his life to Meth. And so, Baal descended into the Netherworld and there stood before Meth. Meth called forth the Anakin Abaddon the Destroyer. Then Mot forced Baal to gaze into the eyes of the destroyer and thus murdered Baal.

Then Anath went to El, at the source of the rivers, in the middle of the bed of the two oceans. She bowed down at the feet of El, she bowed and prostrated herself before him and paid him respect. She spoke and said; "The very mighty Ba'al is dead. The prince, lord of the earth, has died." When God learned of this and he mourned greatly. Coming down from his throne, he sat upon the ground. He strew dust in his hair and wore sackcloth. He rolled in the dirt, weeping. In sorrow, he shaved off his beard and beat his chest in grief. In grief El circumcised himself, compelling his allies also to do the same. Worshipers who are devoted to El also circumcised themselves to show their allegiance to El. He raised his voice and shouted, "Baal is dead. And now what will happen to the peoples of the earth? Dagon's son has departed, what will happen to the masses? I shall go down to the earth in Baal's place." The Counsil of the gods met. They decided, "It is not proper for the God of Heaven to leave the highest heaven to rule on earth. One of us must take Baal's place."

Anath searched for the body of her beloved. Anath sought Baal in the Netherworld. She could not find it anywhere in the depths of Sheol. She lost her patience after her continued search. Then she took hold of the hem of Meth's garment and begged him that he would show her where the body of Baal was. Meth said to Anath, "I will tell you at a price. You must bow before me like the she-dog which you are and allow me to pleasure myself with your body. If you refuse me then you shall never find the body of your beloved Haddad." She acquiesced to his demand and then he told her where he had hidden the body. When she found it, she mourned greatly. Anath took Baal's body to Mount Zaphon and with Shapash prepared his body for burial and led the funeral procession in which his body was taken and entombed in Sheol. The gods and goddesses participated in the funeral rites. Shapash and Anath wept together. Anath covered her loins with sackcloth. She cut her skin with a knife. He made incisions upon her cheeks and chin with a razor. She raked her forearms. She plowed her chest like a garden. She lacerated her back like a valley. Weeping she cried out, "Baal is dead! Woe to the people of Dagon's son! Woe to the multitudes of the servants of Baal! Let us go down into the earth." Anath then made sacrifices for Baal. She sacrificed seventy buffaloes as an offering for Aliyan Baal. She sacrificed seventy oxen as an offering for Aliyan Baal. She sacrificed seventy head of small cattle as an offering for Aliyan Baal. She sacrificed seventy deer as an offering for Aliyan Baal. She sacrificed seventy wild goats as an offering for Aliyan Baal. She sacrificed seventy asses as an offering for Aliyan Baal. And then she was finished with the making of sacrifices.

Behemoth and Leviathan wage war against God

Yam is the physical manifestation or embodiment of the Sea. As long as the Sea endures, Yam endures. And so Meth, the Behemoth, walked upon the coast and spoke to the Sea. And he said, "Yam, my brother, I have vanquished he who vanquished you. Arise and take your form again." And so Yam reconstituted himself and emerged from the water to take counsel with his brother. And Meth spoke to his brother Leviathan and said, "Long ago, it was I who moved the gods against mankind in the Great Flood, to destroy the world of Man, but Elohim frustrated my plans. But now, together, you and I can bring this plan to realization. We can bring it to fruition. Let us destroy the created order established by El. Let us kill God and let there be chaos again as there was in the beginning. Let us avenge ourselves of the murder of our mother Rahab by El and bring down the world that he has made into nothingness. We must act now while to sons of God are without their leader. To revenge our mother, let us unleash an unending chaos, to cause the annihilation all the living and to destroy life and order forever, to destroy every man and animal, all plants and indeed all living things, and to cause all of existence to cease, to do this we must kill our father Elohim." And the plan of the Behemoth was pleasing to his brother Leviathan. The chaos monsters, the sons of Rahab, thus went to war against God.

The Mighty El

Thus, the Leviathan, the Prince of the Sea, and Behemoth, the Great Dragon, the two children of Rahab, arose in rebellion against the Creator of the Universe. The waters of the great deep welled and surged high in their pride to cover the earth. The tremendous billows of the sea lifted up their voice and roared in tumult. The rivers and the streams joined in the rebellion and over flooded their banks. Many helpers, writhing serpents and sea dragons joined with them. But the anger of the Lord God was kindled against all the creatures that revolted against him and he would not turn away in his anger. In his great wrath and in his fury he rose up from his glorious throne and descended from heaven in his anger. He rode upon a cherub and flew riding upon the clouds. He appeared against them in his chariot. He swiftly came upon the wings of the wind. He shouted from heaven and thundered upon the many waters. Yea, with the thunder of his voice he rebuked them. The earth trembled at the sound of his voice. They lifted themselves up but he exalted himself mightily against them. They were mighty, but he was mightier than they. They trembled at the sound of his voice and at the shout of his rebuke. He fought against them with his mighty hand. He smote them with his glorious sword. He beat them with his staff and fired arrows upon them and pierced them with his spear. He broke the heads of the sea dragons and their carcasses sank into the waters. In fear, Yam the Leviathan sank deep within the sea and covered himself with many waters that he might hide from God. And the Lord God made the waters congeal beneath his feet and he walked upon the water as if it were dry ground. He glared at the water and his vision cut through it like a knife and he saw Leviathan. God smote the waters with his staff and they divided. He held his staff over the wavers and they opened a path before him. And El caused the waters to divide before him and the water stood like a wall upon his right hand and at his left. There Leviathan lay exposed before God. And God lay hold of Leviathan. And Leviathan then found himself in the palm of God. He who thought himself mighty before God found that he was altogether less than nothing before El. And God crushed the Leviathan into powder in his fist and threw him back into the sea as if he were garbage and residue of Yam sank like a stone.

In his fury, El then turned to Behemoth and the armies that he had assembled against God. The hosts of Meth, wicked men and monsters and creatures of darkness arrayed themselves against God. And God breathed upon the dragons upon the earth and they withered away and crumbled into dust. God crushed them with his glorious sword. He wounded, pierced and cut off the rebels. As his feet touched the ground the earth split. Many of the villains fell alive into Sheol as the earth opened her mouth to receive them. Other soldiers were consumed by the glory of the presence of Almighty God. Their eyes melted in their sockets. Their tongues withered within their mouths. Their skin rotted off of their body and their bones decayed into dust. God trod upon them and crushed them beneath his feet like grapes. They became the winepress of his fury. Meth was shocked to discover that while the Tablets of Destiny controlled the fates of men and the sons of God, it had no power against God himself. He was then seized with terror and trembled greatly. El grasped Behemoth and lifted him up and threw down his body upon the earth. And Behemoth also ran and fled and hid himself within a mountain. Meth the Behemoth's power is of the earth. He is a chaos monster of earth. It is from the earth that he gains is power. If he is too long removed from the earth he loses his power. Thus he cannot come into the highest heaven and stand before God. So, thus it was into the depths of the earth that he fled from God. El shouted and the earth shook. And the Behemoth and his minions cried out in terror. They cried out to the mountains the rocks and said, "Fall on us!," and to the hills, "Cover us and hide us from the face of he who sits on the throne of glory and from the wrath of Almighty God!" And God caused the earth to shake and split the earth open. The mountains melted before him. The rocks and hills became like wax before him and wasted away. God touched the earth and it melted. The mountains melted before him and the valleys split apart. He lay hold upon Behemoth and wounded and hewed him. He made sport of him and smashed his head. He put a muzzle in Behemoth's mouth and a yoke upon him and enclosed him within the gates of death, deep in the realm of Sheol.

El divides the waters

Thus the rebels were subdued and again God walked upon the seas and trod upon the high places of the earth. God shattered the sea and the mountains. He paraded himself before his enemies to show that he is king. God is the King of Kings and Lord of Lords and he shall reign forever and ever. And all the earth and all the sea were subdued before God Almighty.

And the men of the earth, seeing the mighty exploits of El, praised his holy name. And they sang unto God, saying, "We sing praises to your name, O El Elyon, O God Most High. God is our king from old. He works salvation upon the earth. You, O God, divided the sea by your might, you broke the heads of dragons in the waters. You crushed the heads of the Leviathan; you gave him as food for the animals in the wilderness. Before you, O God, the sea looked and fled. It turned back in horror. You defeated Behemoth. Before God, the mountains skipped like rams and the hills like lambs. You established the stars, the moon and the sun, you have fixed the bounds of the earth and have made summer and winter. God determines the number of the stars and gives names to all of them. Sing to Elohim, sing praises to his name. Lift up a song to him who rides upon the clouds. By your power, you established the mountains; you are girded with might. You silence the roaring of the seas, the crashing of the waves and the tumult of rebellious men. The mountains crumble before you and are nothing. How awesome are your marvelous acts. Because of your great power, your enemies cringe before you. God is a sun and a shield. He bestows honor and favour upon the righteous. He does not withhold good things from those who are upright. Great is our God, and abundant in power. His understanding is beyond measure. God lifts up the downtrodden but he casts the wicked to the ground. O give thanks to the God of gods, for his steadfast love endures forever. O give thanks to the Lord of lords, for his goodness never ends. Praise ye him, Shamash and Yerikh: praise him, all you shining stars. Praise him, ye heavens of heavens, and ye waters that be above the heavens. Let them praise the name of God Almighty: for he commanded, and they were created. He hath also established them for ever and ever: he fixed their bounds which shall not be passed. Praise the EL SHADDAI from the earth, ye dragons, ye sea-monsters and all deeps: Fire, and hail; snow, and vapours; stormy wind fulfilling his word: mountains, and all hills; fruitful trees, and all cedars: beasts, and all cattle; creeping things, and flying birds! Kings of the earth, and all people; princes, and all judges of the earth: Both young men, and women; old men, and children, all together let them praise the name of ELOHIM: for his name alone is excellent; his glory is above the earth and heaven. O Elohim, from everlasting to everlasting thou art God. "

Athtar attempts to rule in the place of Baal

Seeing that Baal was dead and Behemoth the Usurper was restrained by El, the counsil of the gods met and they asked "Who shall sit in the seat of Baal?" Athtar the Morning Star was chosen. He stated, "I now rule as king. I shall be called Moloch." The word Moloch means "the King."

A feast was held when Athtar the Terrible became king in the place of Baal. At the seventh day of the feast a messenger of Sheol arrived at Mount Zaphon and demanded audience with El. Namtar, the emissary of Sheol, said, "Thus saith Sheol, "Am I not a daughter or El and Asherah? Am I not the Great Queen of the Underworld? Am I not a goddess? Shall I be forgotten and treated with contempt? While I may not ascend Mount Zaphon, I have not been shown proper respect. A portion from the table should have been brought to me and yet was not. Athtar must make amends.'"" El agreed with the words of Sheol and commanded that Athtar was to go to the Netherworld to make amends. Kothar-wa-Khasis prepared Athtar for his journey. He gave him warnings, "There is a danger that you could become unclean in the realm of Sheol and thus become imprisoned with her there. You must not sit in a chair there, nor eat bread or meat, drink beer, nor wash your feet and under no circumstances lay with Sheol. Athtar was given entrance through the seven gates of Sheol. Upon his arrival into the royal court, the servants of Sheol offered him a seat. He refused. Then they offered him beer and set before him meat and bread. He politely declined to partake. Finally, Sheol appeared before him in a transparent gown. She stripped before him and offered to wash his feet. He refused to allow her to wash his feet. Then she stripped and bathed before him. Finally, she broke his resistance and he ravished her. For six days he had sexual intercourse with Sheol. Upon the seventh day Athtar the Shining One ascended a shining staircase and returned to heaven.

Athtar the Molech

Ashtoreth and Tammuz

Ashtoreth, who is also called Ishtar and Astarte, was the goddess of lust and carnal pleasure. She eagerly satisfied her own sensual desires and was not the goddess of marriage or childbirth, nor of enduring love, but merely of lust, fleeting passions and sexual pleasure. She possessed a voracious sexual appetite that could not be satisfied. Her lust for sexual pleasure was insatiable. Her symbol was the lion due to its ferocity and destructiveness. She was often seen with Ariel, God's lion, who served as her guardian. Ashtoreth could be selfish and cruel and she was chiefly concerned with satisfying her vociferous sexual appetite and could be very treacherous. Her relationships with men were short and her lovers were legion. Many of them, such as Tammuz, paid a terrible price for giving her their love.

Ashtoreth journeyed to a pleasant valley that was well watered. There she saw a farmer plowing his field. She compelled him to have sex with her. While she was in the throws of passion, she heard the sound of a shepherd playing his reed pipe afar off. She looked and noticed Tammuz at a distance. She saw that he was large, strong and handsome. She left the farmer sleeping on bails of hay and left in pursuit of Tammuz. She then went to the sheepfold to the shepherd. She sat down under an apple tree. She leaned against it and pulled up her skirt and exposed her private parts to Tammuz as he walked by. She offered him her sexual pleasures, he availed himself of them and they courted and spoke to each other of their love.

A father sacrifices his son to Molech

Tammuz the Good Shepherd

Ashtoreth: Let him kiss me with the kisses of his mouth: for thy love is better than wine. Because of the savour of thy good ointments thy name is as ointment poured forth, therefore do the virgins love thee. Tell me, O thou whom my soul loveth, where thou feedest, where thou makest thy flock to rest at noon: for why should I be as one that turneth aside by the flocks of thy companions?

Tammuz: If thou know not, O thou fairest among women, go thy way forth by the footsteps of the flock, and feed thy kids beside the shepherds' tents.

Ashtoreth: A bundle of myrrh is my well-beloved unto me; he shall lie all night betwixt my breasts. My beloved is unto me as a cluster of henna flowers in the vineyards of Engedi.

Tammuz: Behold, thou art fair, my love; behold, thou art fair; thou hast doves' eyes.

Ashtoreth: Behold, thou art fair, my beloved, yea, pleasant: also our bed is green. The beams of our house are cedar, and our rafters of fir. I am the rose of Sharon, and the lily of the valleys.

Tammuz: As the lily among thorns, so is my love among the daughters.

Ashtoreth: As apple tree among the trees of the wood, so is my beloved among the sons. I sat down under his shadow with great delight, and his fruit was sweet to my taste. He brought me to the banqueting house, and his banner over me was love.

Tammuz: Behold, thou art fair, my love; behold, thou art fair; thou hast doves' eyes within thy locks: thy hair is as a flock of goats, that appear from mount Gilead. Thy teeth are like a flock of sheep that are even shorn, which came up from the washing; whereof every one bear twins, and none is barren among them. Thy lips are like a thread of scarlet, and thy speech is comely: thy temples are like a piece of a pomegranate within thy locks. Thou hast ravished my heart, my sister, my spouse; thou hast ravished my heart with one of thine eyes, with one chain of thy neck. How fair is thy love, my sister, my spouse! How much better is thy love than wine and the smell of thine ointments than all spices! Thy lips, O my spouse, drop as the honeycomb: honey and milk are under thy tongue; and the smell of thy garments is like the smell of Lebanon. A garden enclosed is my sister, my spouse; a spring shut up, a fountain sealed. Thy plants are an orchard of pomegranates, with pleasant fruits; camphire, with spikenard, spikenard and saffron; calamus and cinnamon, with all trees of frankincense; myrrh and aloes, with all the chief spices: A fountain of gardens, a well of living waters, and streams from Lebanon.

Ashtoreth: Awake, O north wind; and come, thou south; blow upon my garden, that the spices thereof may flow out. Let my beloved come into his garden, and eat his pleasant fruits. My beloved is white and ruddy, the chiefest among ten thousand. His head is as the most fine gold, his locks are bushy, and black as a raven. His eyes are as the eyes of doves by the rivers of waters, washed with milk, and fitly set. His cheeks are as a bed of spices, as sweet flowers: his lips like lilies, dropping sweet smelling myrrh. His hands are as gold rings set with the beryl: his belly is as bright ivory overlaid with sapphires. His legs are as pillars of marble, set upon sockets of fine gold: his countenance is as Lebanon, excellent as the cedars. His mouth is most sweet: yea, he is altogether lovely. This is my beloved.

Tammuz: Thy two breasts are like two young roes that are twins. Thy neck is as a tower of ivory; thine eyes like the fishpools in Heshbon, by the gate of Bathrabbim: thy nose is as the tower of Lebanon which looketh toward Damascus. Thine head upon thee is like Carmel, and the hair of thine head like purple; the king is held in the galleries. How fair and how pleasant art thou, O love, for delights! This thy stature is like to a palm tree, and thy breasts to clusters of grapes. I said, I will go up to the palm tree, I will take hold of the boughs thereof: now also thy breasts shall be as clusters of the vine, and the smell of thy nose like apples.

Tammuz looked upon her and fell in love with her. He pledged himself to her. He gave her his heart and told her that his heart, his life, his soul was hers and hers alone to do with whatever she wished. Tammuz promised to satisfy her desires but on the condition that she wed herself to him. She at first hesitated, but then agreed to his demand and they were wed. They spent months together making love among the green pastures. Ashtoreth's blessings made the flocks of Tammuz fertile.

The Mourning for Tammuz

But, without the rains of Baal the land became barren. There was a great dearth that came upon the land. In desperation, King Kirta went to the high place of his city, the place called Tophet, there he caused his son to pass through the fire and sacrificed his newborn son to Moloch in the hopes that such a sacrifice would move Athtar to pity and save mankind.

One day, Tammuz woke up. He was awoken by a troubling dream. He left Ashtoreth sleeping as he went to follow his flock. As he walked he came upon the vineyard of his sister Geshtinanna. He rejoiced to see her and they embraced. Afterwards, he told her of his dream which had given him a sense of terrible foreboding. In the dream, gullah-demons, evil spirits that drag the souls of the departed to the realm of Sheol pursued him and dragged him into a place of darkness. Hearing of these dreams troubled Geshtinanna as well.

Ashtoreth woke up and found that Tammuz was not at her side. She desired to feel the pleasures of a man's body. Since Tammuz wasn't present she sought another man to satisfy her cravings. The valley seemed deserted so she departed from it. She grew so tall that her head reached into the clouds. With each step she transversed a thousand fields. Finally, she spied a village. She noticed a settlement of men and she shrank down to normal human size. Walking the streets, she said to the first man she came upon, "Lay with me." The man lay with her. Afterwards she was angry, "Are you a man or a boy? You are weak. I should destroy you. I am a goddess. How dare you not love me with all your strength?" But the man begged for his life, "Spare me, O goddess! I am weak because I haven't had food to eat for over a week for there is a great famine. Have mercy upon me!" Ashtoreth responded, "I shall see if your words are true. If they are not I shall return and destroy you!" She left and walked the streets looking for another man to seduce. As she wandered about, she found only desolation. Emaciated people approached her, "O goddess, have mercy! Baal has withheld his rains and there is a great famine. The furrows in El's fields have dried. Baal has neglected the neglected the furrows of his plowed land. Where is Baal the Conqueror? Where is the prince, the lord of the earth? Why has he withheld his rains?" Women approached Lady Ashtoreth. One said, "O goddess, only months ago I had pretty eyes and a beautiful figure, but now my eyes have sunken into my head and my skin cleaveth unto my bones." Ashtoreth answered her, "That is too bad for you." Another brought her child to Ashtoreth and said, "Look upon my son. Due to the famine he is malnourished and now he is diseased and sickly. I fear that he is not long for this world." Ashtoreth answered her, "I am sorry for you, I really am, but that is your problem and not mine." Yet another woman came to Ashtoreth and said, "Due to the famine, our strong men are brought low and our mighty men are wasting away." At this, Ashtoreth was alarmed. She looked upon the men-folk and saw that they were perishing. Then she spoke, "If all the men perish, with whom shall I find satisfaction? I will not tarry here with you. I shall now arm myself and bring deliverance unto you all."

A great famine came upon the land

Ashtoreth had been in the watered valley with Tammuz and was unaware of the famine. She looked and noticed that there was suffering, starvation and death. She realized that without Baal sending his life giving rains, there was a great dearth upon the earth. People were starving and dying and fewer were engaging in lovemaking and there were fewer men for her to use to satisfy her desires. At this became concerned and decided that she would release Baal from his captivity in the domain of Sheol. But she feared to go alone. She took along her daughter named Karen-Happuch-meaning "Bottle of Make-up." She went to the Garden of God where she had abandoned her. When Karen-Happuch saw her mother she rejoiced, "Mommy! Where have you been?" She answered her, "Honey-cakes, you know that I love you very much but I have been very busy and that is why you haven't seen me for many months." Ashtoreth girded herself with her enchanted armor and magical weapons. Ashtoreth and Karen-Happuch entered the secret corridor at Mount Targhizizi that led to the netherworld. She left Karen-Happuch at the gate of Sheol and told her to wait there. She gave her instructions to go to El her father so that he would rescue her if she did not return upon the third day. Meth saw Ashtoreth enter into his gates so he went and notified his wife Sheol. "Should I send Horon and the armies of the dead to capture her?," he asked. She commanded him to have her remove an article of armor or clothing at each of the seven gates as a payment for passage. At the first gate she removed her helmet, at the second gate she removed her sandals, at the third gate she removed her breastplate, at the fourth gate she removed her robe, at the fifth gate she removed her jewelry, at the sixth gate she removed her shield, at the seventh gate she removed her sword and she was brought into the presence of Sheol, her sister, naked and powerless. Without her enchanted weapons and armour, she was divested of her power.

Then the Annakin named Abaddon the Destroyer approached Ashtoreth. (The Greeks called Ashtoreth Astarte and called Abaddon Apollyon.) Looking into her eyes with his eyes of fire he sucked her soul from her body and imprisoned her soul within a band upon his wrist. He then took her corpse and slung it across the room onto a hook protruding from the wall and there it hung like a slab of meat.

Karen-Happuch waited at outside of the gates of hell until the third day. Then she ran to the Mountain of God and approached her grandfather El. She pled with him, saying, "O Father El, do not let your daughter be put to death in the netherworld. Do not let your princess be covered with the dirt of the underworld. Do not let your precious jewel be shattered in the pit." El cried out, "What happened? What has my daughter done? I am grieved and troubled greatly. Without Ashtoreth all love-making will cease and all life will pass away. And as for Anath, she has also vanished in mourning for Baal. Who knows what has become of her?" Karen-Happuch told El of what she knew of what had happened. Then El said, "Call to Elisha, the carpenter god, Elisha, who built Baal's house which now stands vacant." So Ptah was brought before him. And El spoke to Elisha and said, "Listen, Elisha, carpenter god, go into Sheol and retrieve Ashtoreth my daughter and bring her to me."

Elisha/Ptah/Kothar-wa-Khasis

And so Ptah descended into the Netherworld and he found Sheol in her hall weeping. (Since he was El's envoy he was granted passage. Ptah is also a chthonic deity. He carried the Staff of God to show that he had been sent by God.) She was weeping over her loss of Athtar. Ptah spoke comforting words to her. Ptah planted within her mind a scheme that would result in her being joined with Athtar again. Sheol said that as a reward for his compassion, he may take a gift of his liking from her domain. Ptah pointed to Ashtoreth's body that was hanging like a piece of rotting meat upon the wall.

Sheol

Sheol stated that Ashtoreth would be released from her domain only if a proper substitute could be found. Ptah took Ashtoreth's body down and washed it with the water of life. Ptah found Abaddon and told him that it was El's command that he release Ashtoreth's soul and seeing that Ptah held the Staff of God in his hand, Abaddon did so. Then Ptah told Ashtoreth of Sheol's demand. She could be released only upon the condition that she offer up a substitute. But who? Would she offer up one of her own daughters in her place? Then Ashtoreth remembered the pledge that Tammuz had given her-that his life and his very soul was hers to do with and she pleased and promptly she decided to offer up Tammuz as her substitute. Ashtoreth then fastened the eye of death upon Tammuz. She spoke against him and cried out to Sheol, "Take Tammuz!" Immediately, Sheol sent one of her gullah-demons out in the form of a wild boar. The wild boar pursued Tammuz. He fled to his sister Geshtinana who was nearby. She attempted to hide him but who could not in the end stand up to the demon. Tammuz looked up and saw Shammash driving his Chariot of Fire across the sky. Tammuz cried out to the sun, "Oh Shamash, god of justice, grant me justice and save me!" Shamash heard Tammuz's cry and answered him, "I will save you." But at that moment Tammuz was killed, gored to death, by the wild boar. The boar gored him in the groin, severing his artery. His blood splattered upon the earth. Where his blood dripped, anemone flowers immediately grew. His body fell into the Adonis River which turned red with his blood. From then until this very day, the Adonis River turns red every year at the season in which Tammuz was killed. The gullah demon fished his body out of the river and then dragged the body of Tammuz into the Netherworld to present it to Sheol. When Sheol received the body of Tammuz, she released Ashtoreth. Ashtoreth averted her eyes, so that she would not see the corpse of her husband. As she departed she collected her clothing, her jewelry, her armor and her weapons and left as if nothing had happened.

When Tammuz was taken from his flock, his loyal black sheepdog wailed for him, as did his sheep and the people of the villages near the area where he kept his flock. And there was great mourning for Tammuz, for he was greatly loved, especially by the women, for he had many lovers. The green pastures had become brown and dry when Tammuz departed because they were made green by his blessing. Geshtinanna wept for her brother. She went to Mount Zaphon and searched out the matter and was sore displeased. She said, "I will find my brother. I will comfort him and I will share his fate." She journeyed to Sheol. She called out to her from outside the gates of death and offered herself in the place of her brother. Sheol answered her and said that Tammuz was chosen by Ashtoreth and only Ashtoreth could determine who her substitute was to be. Geshtinana then returned to the surface of the earth on her quest to settle the matter. Geshtinana cried out to Shamash as he flew past in the sky in his chariot of fire which was carried by six winged horses. "Oh Shamash!," she called out, "Fulfill your word and save Tammuz." And Shamash spoke with his wife, Shapash, the goddess of light, who was with him in the chariot. They decided that Shapash would come and assist Geshtinana in her quest for justice. Shapash leaped from the chariot of the sun and took her place by the side of Geshtinanna. And together they sought for Ashtoreth.

Shapash the Solar Goddess

They found her in a far country in a region that had not yet been profoundly affected by the drought. She was in a tavern, laying on a table naked offering herself to all the men in the tavern. Many have availed themselves of her and others stood around waiting for their opportunity. Geshtinana went and asked Ashtoreth if she would speak to her. Ashtoreth refused to come saying that she was busy. Geshtinana then went and brought Shapash into the tavern with her. Shapash then manifested her glory. She glowed with a bright light that filled the tavern. All the men fled in terror. Geshtinana and Shamash then firmly told Ashtoreth, "You will come with us." Ashtoreth came, but not with a willing heart. The three of them went into Sheol and requested audience with the Queen of the Dead. As they walked, Geshtinanna asked Ashtoreth, "Didn't you love, Tammuz? Wasn't he your husband? How could you condemn him to damnation?" The Gates of Hell opened and the three of them entered. Ashtoreth answered, "I must admit, no man pleased me the way Tammuz did." They came into the court of Sheol and stood before her. The body of Tammuz was brought before them all. Ashtoreth again averted her gaze. Ashtoreth became angry that she was dragged away from her pursuit of pleasure and was being forced to make decisions and was being held accountable for her actions. Her one concern was escaping Shapash and Geshtinanna and returning to her sexual exploits. She looked at anger at Geshtinanna, "You can go to hell, since you love him so much." But then she looked upon Shapash, who firmly glared at her. Then she called out to Tammuz, her husband, "You shall go to the Netherworld for half the year, your sister, since she has asked, will go the other half. On the day you are called is the day on which you shall be taken, and on the day Geshtinanna is called, on that day you shall be set free." Then Sheol spoke, "It is hereby declared an arrangement is made by which Geshtinana will take Dumuzid's place in Sheol for six months of the year: You, Tammuz, half the year. Your sister Geshtinanna, half the year!" Accepting the arrangement, Shapash turned to leave but Sheol attempted to detain her. Sheol said, "Halt! Tammuz, Geshtinanna and Ashtoreth have entered a covenant with death-but what of you? You have entered my domain and you may not leave" Shapash then offered to gamble for her release. Sheol agreed to her request and they cast lots. Shapash won her freedom. Geshtinana is the goddess of wine and so she became the goddess of the winter months as well, as this the time in which she is free and Tammuz is imprisoned in Sheol. In the spring and summer, Tammuz is free. As summer ends, Tammuz is mourned as he returns to Sheol.

Upon securing her substitutes and being freed from Sheol, Ashtoreth, who is called Ishtar, had a temple of love built for herself at Baalbek. Any man could come to the temple and make love to the goddess in exchange for a small offering. By engaging in such worship, the man gained the blessing of virility and the act stimulated the forces of life and fertility in the universe. The hope was that by participating in the worship they could stimulate fertility and fecundity. Many men came to engage in such worship so much so that Isthar supplied her priestesses as sacred prostitutes to meet the demand.

Athtar the Morning Star Falls

Several months after their encounter, Sheol again sent Namtar to El with a message, "The seed of Athtar the Awesome is within me and I long to sleep with him again." She threatened El that she would revive all the dead, over whom she ruled, and send them back to earth so that they will outnumber the living unless Athtar was send back to her, for ever, as a husband. She sent a message to Athtar saying, "'Though thou hast climbed up to the heavens, from there I will bring thee down. I shall bring thee down with them that descend into the Pit, I will make sure that you go straight to the Pit, into the lowest part of the earth, into the darkest depths, where you'll be with people who lived in ancient times. I will cause thee to dwell there with the dead, those who have gone into Sheol." Having broken the clear instructions of El as given to him by Ptah, Athtar was forced to descend into the Realm of Sheol. Athtar smashed through the seven gates of death and marched into the great hall of Sheol. He confronted her and laughed in her face as he grabbed her by her hair and pulled her off of her throne. Sheol begged for her life, "Please don't kill me. Listen to what I have to say. Be my husband and I shall be your wife. We shall be king and queen here. Marry me and share in the kingdom that I rule." At her words, Athtar relaxed his grip. And then he embraced her passionately. He drew her close and kissed her, wiping away her tears. He said to her, "You have waited for me and now I have come." And so Athtar fell from heaven and came to rule over hell. Sheol, the domain of the dead, moved at his coming. It aroused for Athtar the spirits of the dead, all the former rulers of the earth; it raised all the departed kings of the nations from their thrones. All the spirits of the kings who had ruled over earth came and greeted Moloch and he became their king. They all respond and said to Athtar, 'Even you have been made as we, you have become like one of us." They were the Milcom, the defied souls of kings of old, who had died, and Moloch became their leader. The royal courts of earth would worship the Milcom and attempt to curry their favor and receive blessings from them.

And a dirge was sung for Athtar, "Thy pomp is brought down to the grave. The worm is spread under thee, and the worms cover thee. How art thou fallen from heaven, O Lucifer, son of Shachar the god of dawn! How art thou cut down to the ground, which didst triumph over the nations! Yet thou hast been brought down to hell, to the sides of the pit."

Asherah came unto El and said unto him, "Athtar attempted to rule in the place of Baal Hadad and yet it seems that the throne of Baal was too big for him. What shall be done now?"

El seated upon his throne

Anath approaches El, her Father

Some time after Athtar fell the Watchers approached El and brought before him the cries of mankind who were suffering due to the famine. El's heart was moved with pity and compassion for mankind.

Since the death of her brother, Anath had been in mourning for him. After Athtar fell, she heard of it and was compelled to act. Anath approached her father El and bowed down low before him and grabbed his legs. "Oh father," she cried, "what hope is there without Haddad? Death will rule over all the earth, for he bears the Tablets of Destiny." (She knew that Meth had the Tablets because Baal had told her before he died.) She wept in his lap. "My child," he said, comforting, "do not cry. Remember, it is I who forged the Tablets of Destiny. They have no power over me. And I declare that your love and ambition are not bound by fate. Lay down at my feet, and wait as I sleep. I shall dream of Baal." After several days he woke up. Anath had waited the whole time. He spoke to her, "I am God Most High. All that I will to be is. As you know, no one can go against the word of God. In the night vision I have looked into the future and I have seen that Baal shall live again. It shall be so. Now go! I lay my hands upon you and endow you with power. Go into Sheol and confront Meth. Demand that he free my son Haddad. Now, go forth and awaken Shachar. Tell him that a new day is dawning."

Anath

Anath brutally kills Mot, grinds him up and scatters ashes

Leaving the presence of El, Anath leapt up and soared through the heavens. She flew across the night sky, shooting across the sky like a red comet. As she struck Mount Tharumagi, the earth shook. The impact awoke Shachar and his light began to shine. She tunneled through the earth as she made her way to Sheol. She stood outside of the Gates of Hell and cried out demanding Haddad from Meth. She was ignored. In fury, she burst through the seven gates of Sheol. Meth called upon Horon the Lord of the Armies of the Dead. Horon sent his soldiers against Anath but she destroyed them all. The demon hoards of Horon attacked Anath but she laid waste to them. The soldiers of death fell before her as wheat falls before a scythe. Anath fought with the fury and strength of a mighty warhorse. Anath saw Horon and challenged him. She said, "Horon, long have I desired to test your fighting prowess in combat. Come and fight me! Let us do battle!" Anath fought Horon. At last Horon fell before her. She killed all the yellow skinned guardians of Meth that stood in her way until she finally arrived at the throne room of Athtar and Sheol. Blocking her way stood Meth. Meth then showed Anath the body of Baal, which was laying in state before the thrones of Sheol his wife and Athtar her husband. Meth said to Anath, "Have you come to beg this of me?" Anath answered, "I am done with begging. You will give me what I demand or I will destroy you." Meth laughed contemptuously at Anath in response. Then Meth spoke to Anath, "Here is the remains of him who you seek. To pass by the gates of Death and enter into the hall of Sheol you must remove all of your armor." "Fine," said Anath as she stripped naked. Then Meth said to her, "And now, you must gaze into the eyes of the destructor! Come forth- Abaddon the Destroyer!" Abaddon approached Anath. "How charming. An Anakin.," said Anath derisively. "Look into my eyes!," demanded Abaddon. "No, you will look into my eyes!," said Anath as she grabbed him by the wrist. She crushed his wrist as if it were a twig and in the process she destroyed his enchanted wristband and released all the souls imprisoned within. She then grabbed his head and said to Abaddon, "Look into the eyes and feel the hands of she who has killed ten thousands of the sons of Anak!" She then thrust her thumbs through the eyes of Abaddon and then crushed his head as if it were a melon. She then tore his head off of his body, threw it to the ground and kicked it across the hall as if it were a ball. Then she turned to Meth and clinched her hand into a fist and approached him. "I don't need my armor and weapons to fight the likes of you." She then struck him in the chest and he flew from the impact and struck the wall. The Gates of Death shook. Meth fell down at the feet of Anath unconscious. And Anath said triumphantly, "Love is stronger than death." Athtar and Sheol then fled away and hid in a secret chamber. Anath seized Meth and attacked him with her sword. She shook him, burned him and crushed him. She ground him into a powder and put his ashes in a sack.

Anath battles an Anakim and the yellow skinned guards

Baal Lives!

Anath approached the remains of her beloved-of Baal the Conqueror. She stood over his cold form which was lying in state. She wept. Her tears fell upon his face. She mounted his body and pressed her body upon his. The warmth of her body revived the body of Haddad. Since death was destroyed she was able to restore him to life. They made love.

Anath arose and praised Elohim. She sang, "God is my strength and power: and he maketh my way perfect. He maketh my feet like hinds' feet: and setteth me upon my high places. He teacheth my hands to war; so that a bow of steel is broken by mine arms. Thou hast also given me the shield of thy salvation: and thy gentleness hath made me great. Thou hast enlarged my steps under me; so that my feet did not slip. I have pursued mine enemies, and destroyed them; and turned not again until I had consumed them. Thousands fell at my left hand and tens of thousands at my right and yet I did not fall. And I have consumed them, and wounded them, that they could not arise: yea, they are fallen under my feet. For thou hast girded me with strength to battle: them that rose up against me hast thou subdued under me. Thou hast also given me the necks of mine enemies, that I might destroy them that hate me. They looked, but there was none to save; even unto God, but he answered them not. Then did I beat them as small as the dust of the earth, I did stamp them as the mire of the street, and did spread them abroad. It is God that avengeth me, and that bringeth down the people under me. And that bringeth me forth from mine enemies: thou also hast lifted me up on high above them that rose up against me: thou hast delivered me from the violent man. Blessed be God my strength which teacheth my hands to war, and my fingers to fight: My goodness, and my fortress; my high tower, and my deliverer; my shield, and he in whom I trust; who subdueth my people under me. Happy is that people, that is in such a case: yea, happy is that people, whose God is ELOHIM. Therefore I will give thanks unto thee, O GOD, and I will sing praises unto thy name."

Anath returned to the surface of the earth carrying the bag with the ashes and ground remains of Meth and threw his remains to the birds and spread them out upon the fields as if she were a farmer sowing seed.

Baal remained in Sheol sleeping. Meth then reconstituted himself. He returned to Sheol and girt himself. There in Sheol he found Baal sleeping. Supposing him to still be dead, he gloated over his body. Then to his surprise, Baal opened his eyes, tore the Tablets of Destiny from off of the chest of Meth and then stuck him with both of his weapons, with both Yagrush and with Aymur. When Meth came to, Baal had disappeared.

Baal-Hadad returns to Mount Saphon

Baal emerged in triumph from Sheol. He sent out his storm wind, the lightning and thunder to loudly announce his return. Rain once again fell upon the earth. Men rejoiced and cried out, "Baal lives! Praise Baal! Baal is king!" Baal journeyed into the wilderness, collapsed and fell asleep. The rains ceased. Due to the rains, everyone was aware that Baal had returned. El commanded Shamash and Shapash to look out for Baal as Shamash rode his chariot across the skies. Men and women also sought for Baal Haddad. People called out "*Jezebel*," meaning "Where is the prince?" or "Where is Baal?" After a long search, Shapash, she who is called "the torch of the gods," spotted him. He was sleeping in the wilderness. Shapash approached him and woke him up with a kiss.

Baal then journeyed to the Mountain of God. Baal approached Elohim and restored unto him the Tablets of Destiny. He did obesience before El and said to him, "Great and marvelous are your deeds, God Almighty. Just and true are you ways, you who are king of all." El, the kind, the compassionate was glad. He opened his mouth and laughed. He raised his voice and shouted, "Now I can sit back and relax; my heart inside me can be at peace; for Baal the Conqueror lives, the prince, the lord of all the earth has been revived. Now Baal will begin the rain season, the season of the wadis in flood; and he will sound his voice of thunder in the clouds and flash his lightening to the earth. " After worshiping his father, he returned to Mount Zaphon, the mountain of his inheritance. There he entered his house and took his place upon his throne. Then he called for the sons of God to meet before him at the Divine Assembly and they all paid him homage, except for Meth, who refused to submit.

Baal-Hadad and Meth engage in combat.

Meth sent a message to Baal, "Fight me. If you do not fight me then I will kill every human being on the earth." Lord Haddad then challenged Meth to hand to hand combat. Whoever was victorious would be king. Meth agreed to fight with Baal. They fought like heroes. At first Meth was winning, then Ba'al was prevailing. The battle went back and forth. They stuck each other with mighty blows. They jumped like horses. They kicked each other like stallions. They gored each other like wild bulls. They bit each other like snakes. The two gods fought upon Mount Zaphon until they were both exhausted. But neither would surrender to the other. Shamash then told Meth that "fighting against Baal is useless because now because El is on Baal side and will overthrow Meth's rule." Upon learning that El favored Baal, Meth became afraid and declared that Baal is king. Ba'al sat on his throne. Haddad was declared the mightiest and once again declared Ayelin, meaning "the victorious."

Baal-Hadad rules again

Baal returned in a triumphal procession to Mount Zaphon and then took his seat upon the throne as king and Anath sat beside him as his consort and queen. The gods assembled. Ashtoreth was discovered to be missing. Shapash, the god's torch, sought for her and found her prostituting herself in the streets. She brought her to the Divine Assembly and made her take her seat among the gods and goddesses. Once all of the *Kadoshim*, El's holy ones, the gods and goddesses, had gathered, El said, "Now, under my authority, Baal rules as king. As long as earth endures, there shall be, summer and winter, springtime and harvest." Baal was victorious. Baal the Conqueror once again ruled as king.

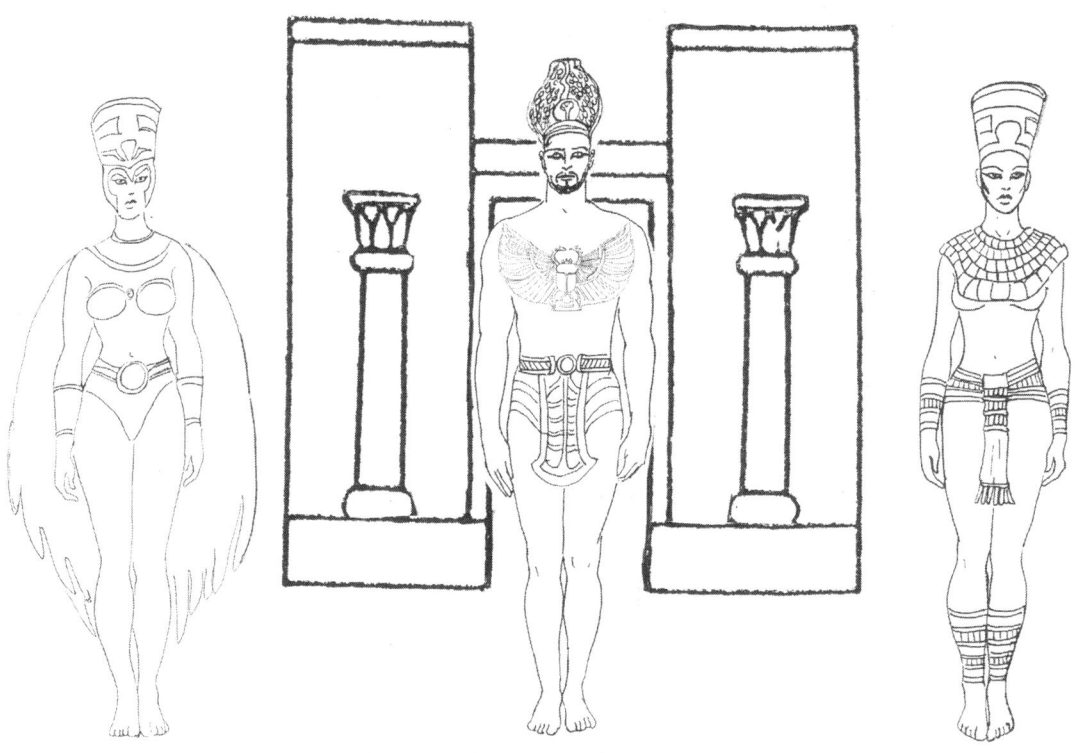

Anath, Haddad and Ashtoreth

Every year the conflict between Lord Haddad and Meth renews, the struggle and the eternal conflict between life and death and the unending battle between good and evil and order and chaos.

And Baal spoke and cried out, "I have a word to tell you, a story to recount to you. The word of the tree and the charm of the stone, the whisper of the heaven to the earth-of the seas to the stars. I understand the lightning, which the heavens do not know, the world which men do not know, and that the earth's masses cannot understand. Come, and I will reveal it in the midst of my mountain, the Holy Mount Zaphon, the pleasant place, the hill I have conquered, in the sanctuary, in the mountain of my inheritance."

THE END

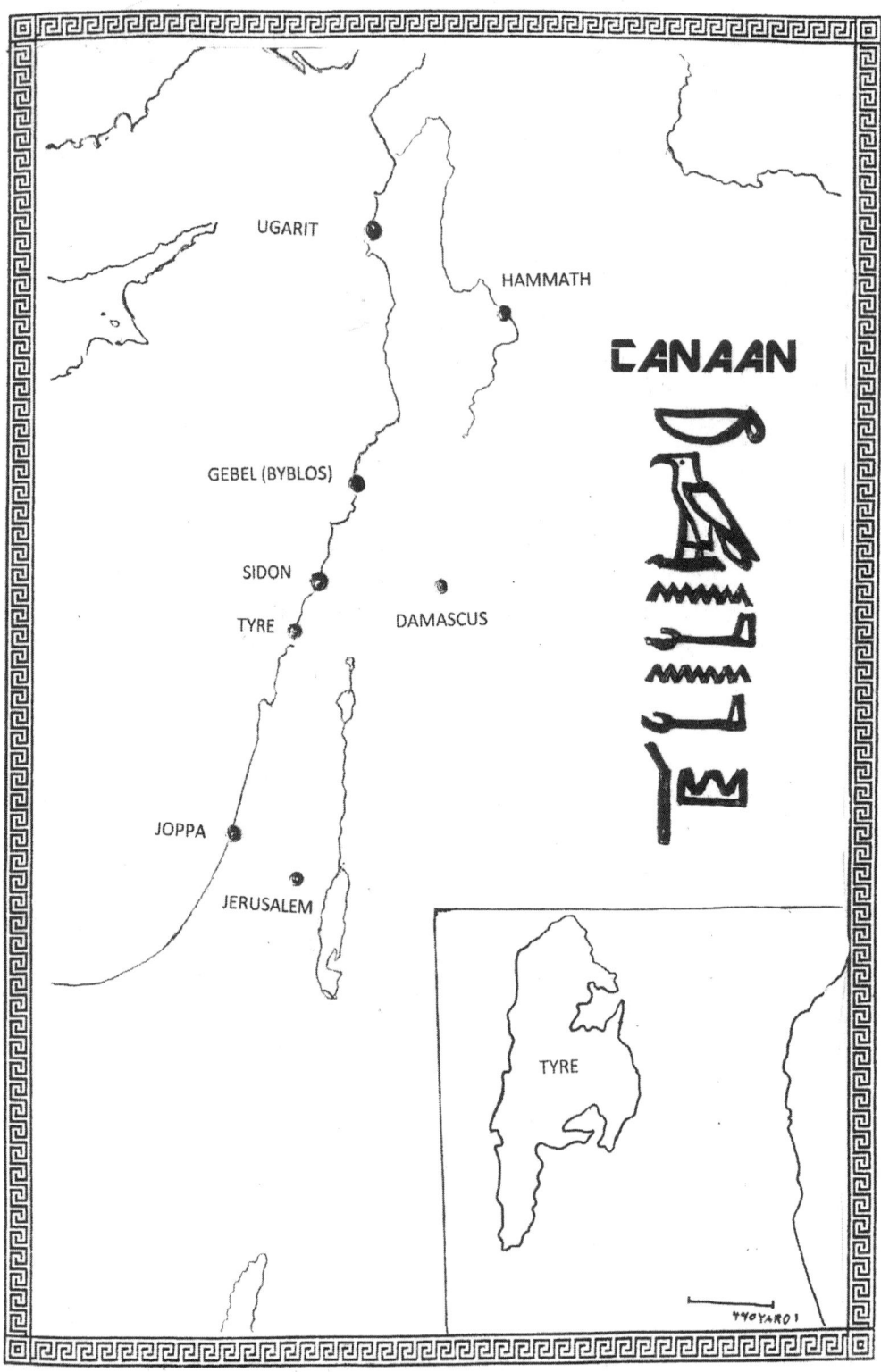

UGARIT

HAMMATH

CANAAN

GEBEL (BYBLOS)

SIDON

TYRE

DAMASCUS

JOPPA

JERUSALEM

TYRE

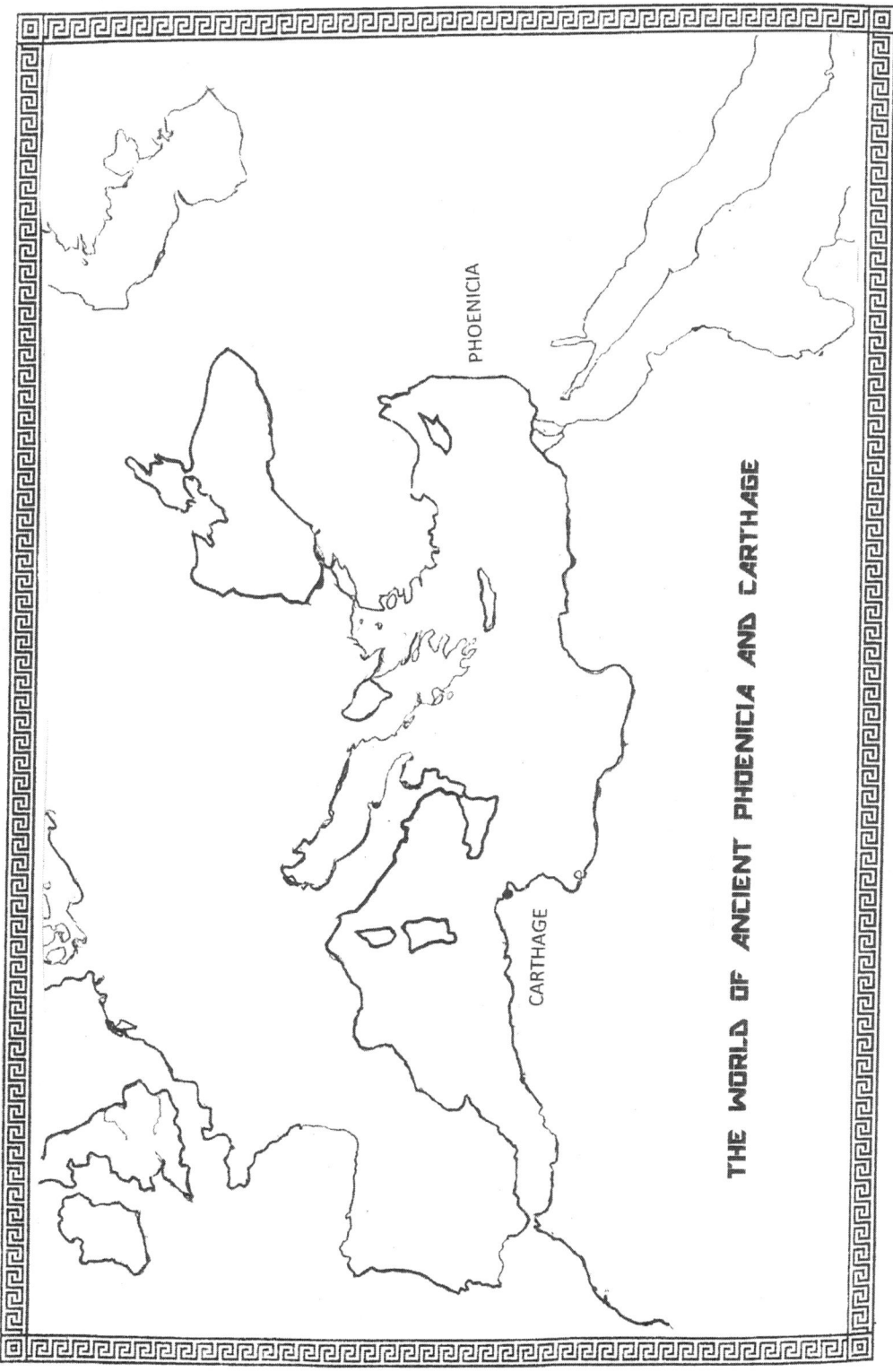

PHOENICIA

CARTHAGE

THE WORLD OF ANCIENT PHOENICIA AND CARTHAGE

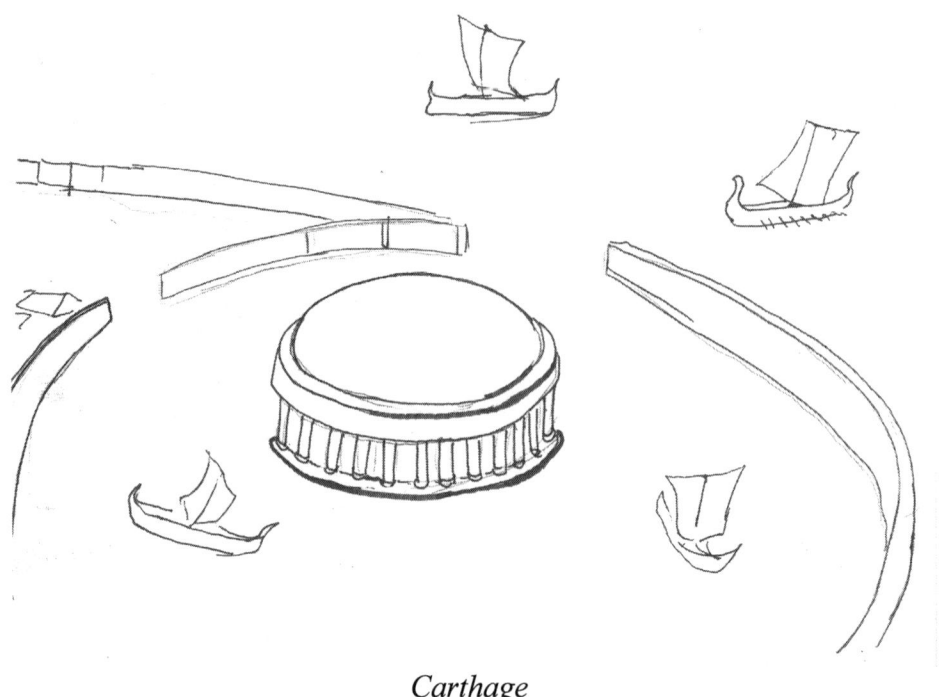

Carthage

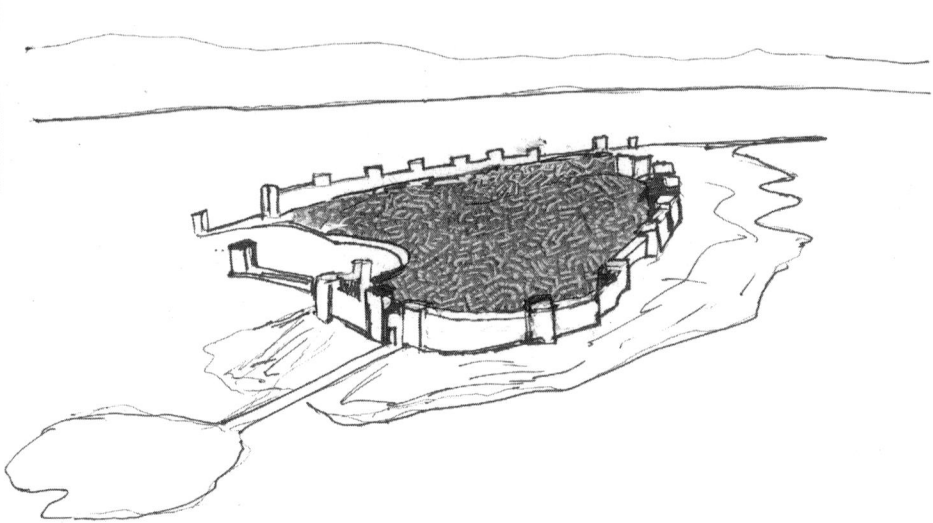

The Isle of Tyre

THE CANAANITE WORLD-VIEW

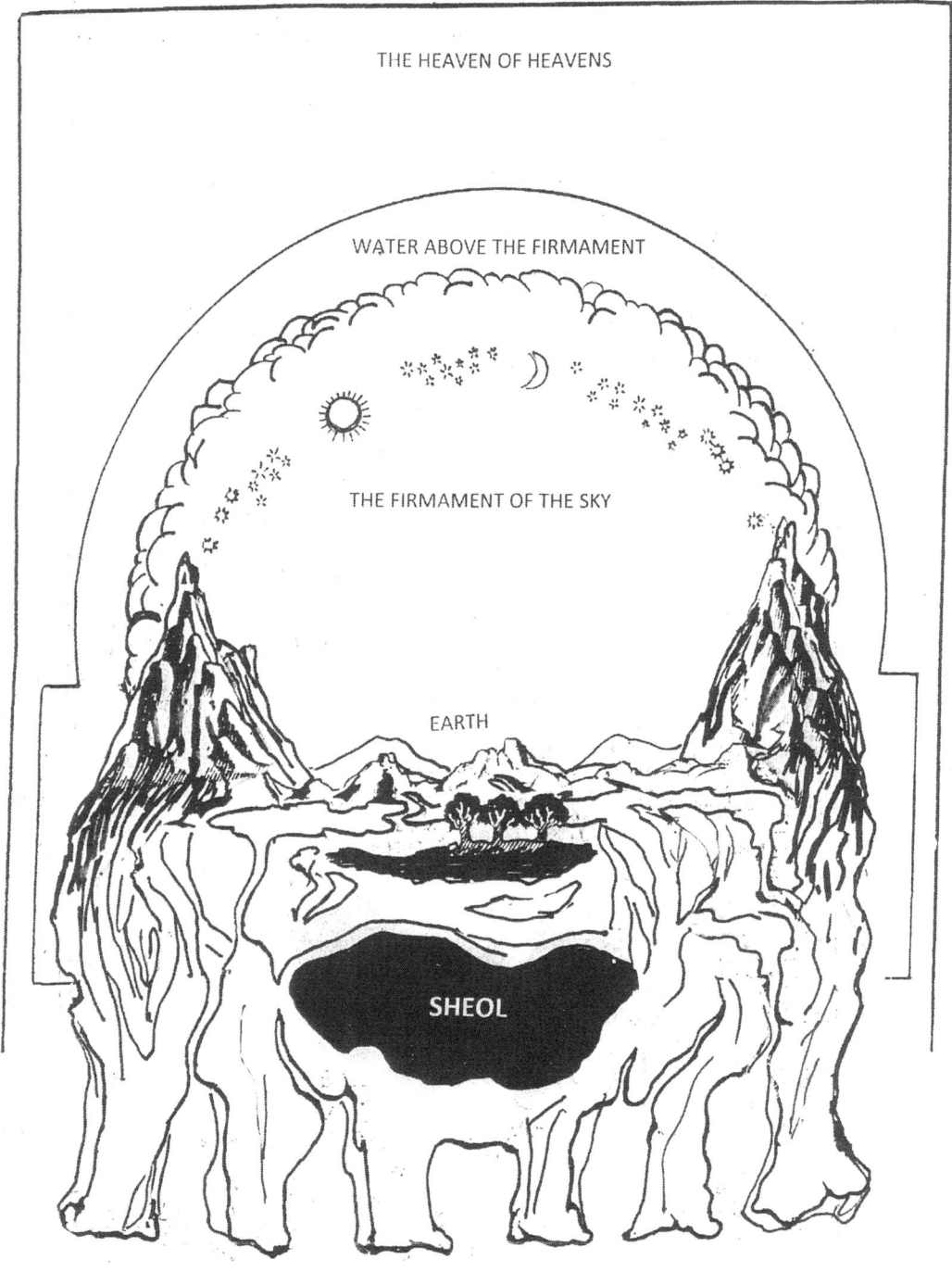

THE HEAVEN OF HEAVENS

WATER ABOVE THE FIRMAMENT

THE FIRMAMENT OF THE SKY

EARTH

SHEOL

Commentary

The Baal Cycle is a companion volume for The Epic of Baal the God of Thunder. In that version, I have extensive commentary. For those who are interested in this subject, I would recommend that you read The Epic of Baal.

Yahweh as Baal/Master

Originally, the name "Baal" meant "Master" or "Lord" or even "husband," which is a meaning and a use that it retains in Modern Israeli Hebrew. King Saul named one of his sons "Ish-Baal," which means "Man of Baal." It is most likely that the "Baal" that Saul was referring to was Yahweh. Even God himself is referred to by David in that way. King David exclaimed "Baal-Perazim"! (2 Samuel 5:20, 1 Chronicles 14:11). He was speaking of Baal Perez, meaning the "Lord of the breakthrough " Baal of the breaches." The context makes it very clear that in this passage Yahweh is called "Baal." 2 Samuel 5:20 reads, "And David came to Baalperazim, and David smote the Philistines there, and said, The LORD [Yahweh in the Hebrew] hath broken forth upon mine enemies before me, as the bursting of flood waters. Therefore he called the name of that place Baalperazim." Isaiah also refers to this at Isaiah 28:21, which says, "For the LORD will rise up as at Mount Perazim." Baal-Perazim is closely associated with Rephaim. We have seen that Baal-Perazim is a place mentioned in the report of the battle between David and the Philistines in II Sam. v. 20 (compare I Chron. xiv. 11). The Philistines encamped in the valley of Rephaim, while David withdrew to the hill-fortress of Adullam and thence proceeded to Baal Perazim, where he defeated the Philistines. Consequently the place must have been situated in the valley of the Rephaim. One of David's mighty men was named Bealiah, which means "Yahweh is Baal" or "Yahweh is Lord" (1 Chronicles 12:5).

Later, the name of Baal came to be largely associated with Baal Haddad and other gods. Yahweh himself states that he was once referred to as Baal by the people of Israel. He says, "Thou shalt call me Ishi ["my husband"]; and shalt call me no more Baali ["my Lord" or "my Baal."]." (Hosea 2:16). So Yahweh spoke to the prophet Hosea, "For I will take away the names of Baalim out of her mouth, and they shall no more be remembered by their name." (Hosea 2:17). This came to pass. The names of the pagan gods and goddesses and their roles came to be largely forgotten until after 1929 when the discoveries at Ugarit in Syria were made.

The Bible says that after settling in the Promised Land, the Israelites "did evil in the sight of the LORD [Yahweh], and forgat the LORD their God, and served Baalim and the groves [Hebrew: Asherim]." (Judges 3:7). What does it mean by the Baalim, meaning the Baals, and the **Asherim**, meaning the Asherahs (or the groves)? We also have the plural form Ashtaroth in Judges 2:13 and 1 Samuel 7:4 where it says, "Then the children of Israel did put away **Baalim** and **Ashtaroth**, and served the LORD only." (see also 1 Samuel 12:10). Ashtaroth is the plural form of Ashtoreth. The singular form is found in 1 Kings 11:5 which states that "Solomon went after Ashtoreth, the goddess of the Zidonians and after Milcom, the abomination of the Ammonites." This means that Solomon became devoted to Ashtoreth and to the Milcom, who are probably the spirits of former kings. As the prophet said, "For *according to* the number of thy cities were thy gods, O Judah; and *according to* the number of the streets of Jerusalem have ye set up altars to *that* shameful thing, *even* altars to burn incense unto Baal." (Jeremiah 11:13).

But why are their Baals and Asthoroths and Asherahs? Concerning Baal, we have seen that different gods were called Baal. Later, it came to be used mainly for Haddad. It is also likely that there was an Ashtoreth of Sidon as there is an "Our Lady of Guadalupe" and an "Our Lady of Fatima" and "Our Lady of Lourdes." There is one Mary, the mother of Jesus, but she has had different manifestations, invocations and titles. The same may be true of Yahweh. In the Bible we have Yahweh of Sinai, Yahweh of Seir and Yahweh of Teman. (Yahweh of Teman has also been found in an extra-biblical inscription in the Sinai.)

Esdras, Behemoth and Leviathon

The ancient Hebrews had a myth about how Yahweh conquered the chaos monsters, Rahab, Behemoth and Leviathan. This story is not found in the Bible, but it is alluded to in several passages of Scripture. A complete account of this ancient Hebrew myth is found in an apocryphal book, which is included in many editions of the Holy Bible. A version of this "Epic of El" is found in 2 Esdras 6:38-53. Which reads, *"My heart vexed within me again, and I began to speak before the most High. For my spirit was greatly set on fire, and my soul was in distress. And I said, O Lord, thou spakest from the beginning of the creation, even the first day, and said thus; Let heaven and earth be made; and thy word was a perfect work. And then was the spirit, and darkness and silence were on every side; the sound of man's voice was not yet formed. Then commandedst thou a fair light to come forth of thy treasures, that thy work might appear. Upon the second day thou madest the spirit of the firmament, and commandedst it to part asunder, and to make a division betwixt the waters, that the one part might go up, and the other remain beneath. Upon the third day thou didst command that the waters should be gathered in the seventh part of the earth: six parts hast thou dried up, and kept them, to the intent that of these some being planted of God and tilled might serve thee. For as soon as thy word went forth the work was made. For immediately there was great and innumerable fruit, and many and divers pleasures for the taste, and flowers of unchangeable colour, and odours of wonderful smell: and this was done the third day. Upon the fourth day thou commandedst that the sun should shine, and the moon give her light, and the stars should be in order: And gavest them a charge to do service unto man, that was to be made. Upon the fifth day thou commandest unto the seventh part, where the waters were gathered that it should bring forth living creatures, fowls and fishes: and so it came to pass. For the dumb water and without life brought forth living things at the commandment of God, that all people might praise thy wondrous works. Then didst thou ordain two living creatures, the one thou calledst Enoch, and the other Leviathan; And didst separate the one from the other: for the seventh part, namely, where the water was gathered together, might not hold them both. Unto Enoch thou gavest one part, which was dried up the third day, that he should dwell in the same part, wherein are a thousand hills: But unto Leviathan thou gavest the seventh part, namely, the moist; and hast kept him to be devoured of whom thou wilt, and when. Upon the sixth day thou gavest commandment unto the earth, that before thee it should bring forth beasts, cattle, and creeping things: And after these, Adam also, whom thou madest lord of all thy creatures: of him come we all, and the people also whom thou hast chosen. All this have I spoken before thee, O Lord, because thou madest the world for our sakes. As for the other people, which also come of Adam, thou hast said that they are nothing, but be like unto spittle: and hast likened the abundance of them unto a drop that falleth from a vessel. And now, O Lord, behold, these heathen, which have ever been reputed as nothing, have begun to be lords over us, and to devour us. But we thy people, whom thou hast called thy firstborn, thy only begotten, and thy fervent lover, are given into their hands. If the world now be made for our sakes, why do we not possess an inheritance with the world? How long shall this endure"* (In this version, which is from the King James Bible, one beast is called Enoch and the other is called Leviathan. However, most scholars believe that, based on textual evidence, it should read, "Then you kept in existence two living creatures; the one you called Behemoth and the name of the other Leviathan." (2 Esdras 6:49, NRSV). (In the creation account in Genesis chapter one, it says that God/Elohim created a "greater light to rule the day and a lesser night to rule the night." This way the biblical writer avoided using the names Shamash for the sun and Yerikh for the moon, as these are the names of pagan gods in the Canaanite pantheon and the goal of the writers of the Bible was to promote monotheism.)

I believe that the story of Moses and the Red Sea crossing was an event that occurred in human history. However, the Hebrews used language that evoked the earlier story of God's conquering the beast of the sea to describe this miraculous event.

The story of God conquering Rahab the chaos-monster is found in Psalm 89:10, Job 26:12 and Isaiah 51:9. Behemoth and Leviathan are mentioned in Job 40:15-41:11. Other references to Yahweh destroying the Chaos-demons are found in Isaiah 27:1, "In that day the LORD with his sore and great and strong sword shall punish leviathan the piercing serpent, even Leviathan that crooked serpent; and he shall slay the dragon that *is* in the sea" and Psalm 74:12-14, "For God *is* my King of old, working salvation in the midst of the earth. Thou didst divide the sea by thy strength: thou brakest the heads of the dragons in the waters. Thou brakest the heads of Leviathan in pieces, *and* gavest him *to be* meat to the people inhabiting the wilderness."

The story of God destroying the chaos monsters is an ancient Hebrew story that did not make it into the Bible. (This is similar to the "Camel of God" Sura that was omitted from the Koran probably when Caliph Omar made changes to the Koran when he standardized the text. This missing sura is still referenced in the Koran.) However, this story was a part of the oral culture of the Jews and thus we find it referenced in the book of 2 Esdras and in the Revelation of Jesus Christ given to Saint John the Revelator.

We also see Hebrew/Canaanite motifs in the Apocalypse genre and even in the Apocalypse in the New Testament. The Book of Revelation refers to a beast from the Sea in Revelation 13:1. It appears with seven heads, as the Leviathan (or Lothan) is portrayed by the Canaanites. In the book of Revelation, we also see the beast from the earth in Revelations 13:11.

Umberto Cassuto in *The Goddess Anath: Canaanite Epics on the Patriarchal Age* discusses the Epic of El in which El destroys the chaos monsters as does J. Day in *God's Battle with the Dragon and the Sea: Echoes of a Canaanite Myth in the Old Testament*.

Joppa and Cassiopeia

In the Greek myth, Cassiopeia, the mother of Andromeda, who was saved from the sea monster Cetus by the hero Perseus, was the queen of Ethiopia. Some ancient authors believed that she ruled over Joppa and that the place-name Joppa was derived from the later part of Cassiopeia's name (meaning that Jopppa came from –iopeia). There are similarities between the story of Perseus and the Kraken and the story of Baal and his destruction of Yam. Many scholars believe that the Perseus story was influenced by the Epic of Baal.

Aurelian and Elagabalus

A short time before Constantine, the Roman Emperor Aurelian attempted to make El the God of the Roman Empire. (Aurelian defeated Queen Zenobia of the Palmyrene Empire in the East.) Aurelian strengthened the position of the Sun god, Sol Invictus or Elagabalus, as the main divinity of the Roman pantheon. (Elagabalus means "El of the Mountain" and is most likely equivalent to El Shaddai.) Aurelian's intention was to give to all the peoples of the Empire, civilian or soldiers, easterners or westerners, a single god they could believe in without betraying their own gods. The center of the cult was a new temple, built in 274 in *Campus Agrippae* in Rome, with great decorations financed by the spoils of the Palmyrene Empire. Aurelian did not persecute other religions. However, during his short rule, he seemed to follow the principle of "one god, one empire", that was later adopted to a full extent by Constantine. On some coins, he appears with the title *Deues et dominus natus* ("God and born ruler"), also later adopted by Diocletian. Lactantius argued that Aurelian would have outlawed all the other gods if he had had enough time. Aurelian attempted to promote the worship of the Semitic Canaanite/Syrian god El the supreme god of the Roman Empire. Later, Constantine endeavored to make the worship of the Semitic Hebrew/Jewish God Elohim/Yahweh the dominate religion of the Roman Empire which did eventually come to pass. Before Aurelian promoted the worship of Elagabalus, it was promoted by Emperor Marcus Aurelius Antoninus, who is commonly called Elagabalus after his deity. His efforts to promote the worship of Elagabalus were a great failure. Vicious rumors of his bi-sexuality and perversity were recorded by Roman historians but they may be character assassination that was a reaction to his unpopular religious innovations. He was assassinated in 222 AD. Decades later, in 274 the Roman Emperor Aurelian made Elagabalus/Sol Invictus an official cult of the Roman state alongside the traditional cults. He was assassinated in 275 AD. (For more information see "Constantine the Emperor" by David Potter.)

The Rephaim and Ancestor Worship in Ancient Israel

In "The Epic of Baal the God of Thunder," I mentioned how that the Israelites practiced worship of their ancestors, the Rephaim. We know that the Israelites were worshiping their ancestors based on excavations of ancient Israelite cemeteries. The Israelites worshiped their ancestors at graves and near to their mortal remains. Now, imagine that you are an Israelite and that you are leaving Egypt, a land that your ancestors lived in for generations. As an ancestor worshiper, this puts you in a difficult position. It is not feasible for you to carry all of the remains of your ancestors with you. So what would you do? In a practical manner and according to the belief system, you don't really have to move all your ancestors anyway, only the patriarchs. And, according to the Bible this is exactly what the Israelites did. You are connected to all of your ancestors through the patriarchs. (When you worship a patriarch, you are connected with all your forefathers that descended from him, through him.) Joseph was exhumed. It is likely that it wasn't just Joseph who was exhumed, but all the patriarchs. So we see, not all the graves needed to be moved, only those of the patriarchs. And they were. Taking your father's forefather is enough because he watches over all of his descendents, living and dead and you are connected to all the remains that you were not able to take with you, through him. So we see in Exodus 13:19, "And Moses took the bones of Joseph with him, for he had made the sons of Israel solemnly swear, saying, "God shall surely take care of you; and you shall carry my bones from here with you." This is quiet unusual, seeing all the rules in the Torah regarding the un-cleanliness of the remains of the dead that they would take the mortal remains of an ancestor and carry them with them during the forty years that they spent wandering in the wilderness. Joseph's bones must have been kept in some kind of a mobile shrine.

According to ancient Canaanite custom, as has been illustrated by excavations at ancient Jericho, one's ancestors were buried in one's own house. Sometimes, after some time had passed, the body would be exhumed and the skull would be taken out and coated with plaster to recreate the facial features upon the skull. (I have Aqhat allude to that in the story.) The deceased relatives could watch over the family and bless the family by being buried in the home. It is interesting that the Israelite prophet Samuel was buried according to this ancient Canaanite custom. The Bible says, "And Samuel died; and all the Israelites were gathered together, and lamented him, and buried him in his house at Ramah." (1 Samuel 25:1).

I also mentioned how that the Israelites were a tribe that worshiped El. Moses taught the people that Yahweh was El and was the only God that they were to worship. The challenge for the prophets of Yahweh was that many of the Israelites conceived of El as the Canaanite deity in the Baal pantheon. This is why they struggled with "paganism," the threat wasn't the temptation of adopted the practices of their "pagan" neighbors, it was the attraction of their own ancient ancestoral traditions that the prophets of Yahweh wanted them to reject.

Sheol and the Fall of Athtar

The Hebrews would worship the Elohim, meaning "the gods," the Rephaim, meaning the spirits of their ancestors and the Milcom, the spirits of kings who died.

We know from the Bible, the Ugaritic texts and from archeological excavations, that the Hebrews believed that the spirits of the dead descended into Sheol, the Netherworld. Rachel S. Hallote's *"Death, Burial, and the Afterlife in the Biblical World,"* is an excellent book about the ancient Israelites view of the afterlife. (However, the book contains hateful statements about Messianic Jews, which I found out of place.)

Isaiah 14 has traditionally been understood to be telling the story of the fall of the devil. Some scholars now believe that it is alluding to the Canaanite myth of the fall of Athtar. It seems that the story of the Fall of Satan is found in the Gospel of Luke and in the Revelation of Saint John as some scholars argue that the passages thought to be referring to the story of the Fall of Satan in Ezekiel and Isaiah may have been misinterpreted. Other passages of Scripture that deal with the ancient Hebrews concept of the afterlife are found in Ezekiel 26:20, Jonah 2:2 and 6 and Amos 9:2. Also, we see that King Saul consulted an Israelite witch who was able (according to a straightforward reading of the text) to contact the spirit of the deceased prophet Samuel (1 Samuel 28:3-25).

The Sacred Grove

We find sacred trees from the beginning of the Bible. In Genesis, we find the Tree of Life and the Tree of Knowledge (or perhaps better translated "the Tree of Knowing Right from Wrong."). It seems that in Canaanite thought we find Asherah as the Tree of Life and the Tree of the Knowledge. In the Book of Proverbs, we have the personification of Wisdom speaking in a woman's voice. This figure does seem to have many similarities to Asherah. She is the Tree of Life (Proverbs 3:18) whose fruit brings wisdom (Proverbs 8:19). Abraham lived at the Oak of Mamre, a sacred tree where Yahweh appeared to him (Genesis 18:1). (An angel appeared to Gideon at an oak, according to the Book of Judges. Interestingly, in Greek mythology, dryads were often associated with oaks. In this version of the Baal story, I depict Asherah as a dryad or hamadryad.) And of course, Yahweh appeared to Moses at a Burning Bush, another sacred tree in Exodus 3:1-6).

At Kuntillet 'Ajrud (Horvat Teman), and ancient inscription speaking of Yahweh and His Asherah was discovered. So, who or what is this Asherah? It is the goddess or it is a sacred tree? In this story, Asherah is both. In the pagan Canaanite religion, El's wife was the goddess Asherah, who was worshiped with the sacred tree. The Prophets of Yahweh identified Yahweh with El, but they rejected Asherah worship. Instead of Asherah being the spouse of God, the nation of Israel was. This helps explain a confusing verse in the Bible such as Psalm 52:8, "As for me, I am like a green olive tree in the house of El." The Bible doesn't usually treat of green olive trees in the house of God. In Jeremiah 11:15-16, Yahweh speaks to his wayward wife, symbolized by the aforementioned olive tree. The prophet says, "Therefore pray not thou for this people, neither lift up a cry or prayer for them; for I will not hear them in the time that they cry unto Me for their trouble. What hath My beloved to do in Mine house, seeing she hath wrought lewdness with many, and the holy flesh is passed from thee? When thou doest evil, then thou rejoicest. The LORD called thy name, 'A Green Olive Tree,' fair and of goodly fruit. With the noise of a great tumult He hath kindled fire upon it, and the branches of it are broken." In the Book of the Prophet Zechariah, we see the Menorah, a lamp-stand shaped like a sacred tree that was kept in the sanctuary, with olive trees (Zechariah 4:1-14). There is another interesting passage in Joshua 24:26. Joshua has made a covenant with the people of Israel, that they worship Yahweh alone and put away all the other gods that they had worshiped while the dwelt in Egypt. The Scripture says, "And Joshua wrote these words in the book of the law of God, and took a great stone, and set it up there under an oak, that was by the sanctuary of the LORD." So we see here that there was an oak tree next to the Tabernacle. The oak tree seems to be beside the central tent in the court of the Tabernacle. Here we have an oak tree in the house of God beside the Tabernacle and under this sacred tree, Joshua erects a stone monument commemorating the oath of commitment to Yahweh that the people of Israel had made. Also, the prophetess Deborah prophesied and held court at a palm tree according to the Book of Judges in the Holy Bible.

Who is this Bull El?

As we see in the Ugaritic texts El was often called the "Bull El." The bull was also used as a symbol of a god in Egypt with the Mnevis and Apis bulls. It seems that the "Golden Calf" was a statue of a bull that represented El in some way. When the High Priest Aaron made the Golden Calf he said, "These are your Elohim, O Israel, who brought you up out of the land of Egypt"

(Exodus 32:4). Moses wasn't pleased. (In Nehemiah 9:16-21, Nehemiah in his account of this incident has it as "This is your God (El) that brought you out of Egypt." Aaron says in Exodus 32:4-5, "Tomorrow will be a feast for Yahweh." It seems like Aaron was adopting pagan, or traditional, elements of the worship of El and applying them to Yahweh.) Later, King Jeroboam of Israel, who broke away the northern tribes away from King Rehoboam of Judah, built two Golden Calves, one in Bethel and the other in Dan (1 Kings 12:29). Even devoted a Yahweh worshiper such as King Jehu of Israel, who abolished Baal worship and slaughtered Baal worshipers, was afraid to directly attack the Golden Calves (2 Kings 9-10, 10:28-29). We don't even have records of Elijah and Elisha attacking the Golden Calves at Bethel and Dan. But perhaps they did but those prophecies were not included in the Scripture. However, Hosea did attack and condemn these altars. He says, regarding the Golden Calves, "For from Israel *was* it also: the workman made it; therefore it *is* not God: but the calf of Samaria shall be broken in pieces." Other translations word it differently, but the general sense is the same. In the New English Bible, it is translated as "What sort of god is this bull?" Others have suggested "for who is this Bull El?" is a better reading. (In the Hebrew, God is called "the Bull of Jacob" in Genesis 49:24.)

The Tent of El

In the Ugaritic texts, El is spoken of as dwelling in a tent. In ancient Israelite religion, the Tabernacle was the dwelling place of God. (There seems to be no temple to El at Ugarit. Some have argued that El is Dagan and thus Dagon's temple is El's and others think that the Rhyton Temple at Ugarit is a temple to El. The remains of a Midianite tabernacle, containing a brass serpent, has been discovered by archeologists at Timna.) The prophet Nathan discouraged David from building a Temple to God and in his prophecy stressed that God's dwelling place is a tent (2 Samuel 7:1-17). After the Jews returned from their Babylonian Captivity, a prophecy contained in Isaiah seems to discourage the rebuilding of the Temple (Isaiah 66:1). This opposition to the temple is also found in Revelation, which states that "the Tabernacle of God is now with Man" but that there is no longer any temple in God's holy city (Revelations 21:3, 22). (Revelation contains other ancient Canaanite themes, the struggle against the chaos-beasts of the earth and sea, the Tree of Life finally being made available to all and we see the final defeat of Yam. In the New Heaven and New Earth there is no more Sea, chaos is finally defeated forever (Revelations 21:1). In Ezekiel 23, Ezekiel calls Israel Oholah, which means "she who possesses a tent," and Judah is called "Oholibah," meaning "My [God's] tent is in her." Ezekiel is recognizing that there was a Sacred Tent in Israel but only the "tent" in Jerusalem is the legitimate sanctuary of God. Richard Elliot Friedman in "Who Wrote the Bible" argues convincingly from Scripture that the Tabernacle was kept in the Temple of Jerusalem. I have been to the high place platform at Tel-Dan. Some scholars believe that a "tent of El" was erected over that platform in Tel-Dan.

God and Man

Many people are interested in exploring the Semitic or Jewish roots of Christianity. However, many people in this movement have been co-opted by people who obsess about the supposed "pagan roots" of what they view as "institutional Christianity." They claim that Christianity is derived from "Babylonian Religion." In doing so they betray their gross ignorance about ancient religions. The idea that they have is that Christianity is somehow corrupt and that Judaism is a more "pure" religion. Often, they attempt to in their view "restore" some Jewish elements that they perceive as having been lost or forsaken back into Christianity. If they knew more about paganism, instead of the outdated fraudulent information that they put out, they would realize that the arguments they make of Christianity being derived from paganism could also be made of Judaism.

Since I was constantly being confronted with people in Hebrew/Semitic roots movement and other circles who constantly talked about pagan gods (usually Baal, Nimrod, Semiramis, Tammuz and Mithra) I decided that it was necessary for me to research Canaanite and Babylonian mythology, although, initially these subjects didn't interest me. (I'd rather learn more about theology, developing a prayer life, or evangelism.) Once I learned about Biblical backgrounds regarding the pagan religion, I got an idea to do a series of books on the Exodus story, and explaining Moses cultural background through Egyptian and Canaanite mythology. Moses grew up as an Egyptian and a Hebrew. The Hebrew culture that Moses was exposed to growing up in Egypt, was a pagan one, according to the Bible (Joshua 24:14). In this passage, Joshua says, "Now therefore fear the LORD, and serve him in sincerity and in truth: and put away the gods which your fathers served on the other side of the flood, and in Egypt; and serve ye the LORD." The gods the Israelites were worshiping in Egypt were the gods of Canaan, which the Egyptians also worshiped, along with Egyptian gods. Egyptians worshiped Anath, Reshep, and Qudshu among other Syria/Canaanite gods who were introduced to them by the Semites who settled in Egypt. In the book of Ezekiel it is written, "Thus saith the Lord GOD; In the day when I chose Israel, and lifted up mine hand unto the seed of the house of Jacob, and made myself known unto them in the land of Egypt, when I lifted up mine hand unto them, saying, I am the LORD your God; In the day that I lifted up mine hand unto them, to bring them forth of the land of Egypt into a land that I had espied for them, flowing with milk and honey, which is the glory of all lands: Then said I unto them, Cast ye away every man the abominations of his eyes, and defile not yourselves with the idols of Egypt: I am the LORD your God. But they rebelled against me, and would not hearken unto me: they did not every man cast away the abominations of their eyes, neither did they forsake the idols of Egypt (Ezekiel 20:5-8).

2 Kings 23 is very interesting in its description of all the Canaanite practices that went on in Solomon's Temple, probably for centuries, until these customs were abolished by the righteous king Josiah: "And the king commanded Hilkiah the high priest, and the priests of the second order, and the keepers of the door, to bring forth out of the temple of the LORD all the vessels that were made for Baal, and for the grove [Asherah], and for all the host of heaven [the sons of El]: and he burned them without Jerusalem in the fields of Kidron, and carried the ashes of them unto Bethel. And he put down the idolatrous priests, whom the kings of Judah had ordained to burn incense in the high places in the cities of Judah, and in the places round about Jerusalem; them also that burned incense unto Baal, to the sun [Shamash], and to the moon [Yerikh], and to the planets, and to all the host of heaven [meaning all the other Canaanite gods]. And he brought out the grove [the Asherah pole] from the house of the LORD [YAHWEH], without Jerusalem, unto the brook Kidron, and burned it at the brook Kidron, and stamped it small to powder, and cast the powder thereof upon the graves of the children of the people. And he brake down the houses of the sodomites, that were by the house of the LORD, where the women wove hangings for the grove [Asherah]. And he brought all the priests out of the cities of Judah, and defiled the high

places where the priests had burned incense, from Geba to Beersheba, and brake down the high places of the gates that were in the entering in of the gate of Joshua the governor of the city, which were on a man's left hand at the gate of the city. Nevertheless the priests of the high places came not up to the altar of the LORD in Jerusalem, but they did eat of the unleavened bread among their brethren. And he defiled Topheth, which is in the valley of the children of Hinnom, that no man might make his son or his daughter to pass through the fire to Molech. And he took away the horses that the kings of Judah had given to the sun, at the entering in of the house of the LORD, by the chamber of Nathanmelech the chamberlain, which was in the suburbs, and burned the chariots of the sun with fire. [Apparently, there was a sculpture of Shamash and his horses pulling his chariot of the Sun/Shamash at the entrance to the Temple of Yahweh.] And the altars that were on the top of the upper chamber of Ahaz, which the kings of Judah had made, and the altars which Manasseh had made in the two courts of the house of the LORD, did the king beat down, and brake them down from thence, and cast the dust of them into the brook Kidron. And the high places that were before Jerusalem, which were on the right hand of the mount of corruption, which Solomon the king of Israel had builded for Ashtoreth the abomination of the Zidonians, and for Chemosh the abomination of the Moabites, and for Milcom the abomination of the children of Ammon, did the king defile. And he brake in pieces the images, and cut down the groves, and filled their places with the bones of men. Moreover the altar that was at Bethel, and the high place which Jeroboam the son of Nebat, who made Israel to sin, had made, both that altar and the high place he brake down, and burned the high place, and stamped it small to powder, and burned the grove." The Patriarch Jacob had built the shrine at Bethel and erected a Baetylus there. (Earlier, according to Genesis 12, Abraham had worshiped near Bethel and erected an altar there but in Genesis 28, Jacob puts the stone under his head and has a vision of angels. He then erected the stone and anointed it with oil. Later Jeroboam, first king of Israel, set up centres for his Golden Calf cult at Bethel on the southern boundary of his kingdom and Dan on the northern boundary, and appointed non-Levites as his priests (1 Kings 12:25–33). The "Golden Calves" were probably symbols of El.

There are interesting similarities between the ancient Israelite priesthood and the Egyptian, Canaanite and Carthaginian priesthoods. In Egypt, Canaan and Carthage, their priests would shave their beards and their heads. Korah the priest is mentioned in Exodus 6:21, Numbers 16, 26:11). The name Korah means "bald head," perhaps referring to the shaved head of a priest. (Korah died due to his opposition to Moses but his sons did not die and they continued as Levites to serve as minor priests. Moses required his priests to shave their entire bodies with razors in accordance with the Near Eastern custom (Numbers 8:7).

I remember reading an article about world religions entitled "Man's Search for God." As a Bible-believer, that made me think that the Bible is the story of "God's Quest for Man." It is the story about how God revealed himself to mankind. Apparently, a Jewish rabbi had the same idea and wrote a book with a similar title to that. God revealed himself to people in what many people now would view as a thoroughly pagan culture. God condescended to man and revealed Himself in a way that the ancients could understand.

I read a Bible scholar write that the reason that the Old Testament seems vague about the nature of the Afterlife is because that the prophets were rejecting the obsessive focus on the Afterlife that they saw in Egypt. But the reality is that, it wasn't Egyptian religious practices they were trying to discourage, but the religious practices of their own people. Since care for the dead is such an important issue, the writers chose to in a way avoid the issue. At the time of Jesus, this resulted in two sects of Judaism, the Pharisees, who did believe in the afterlife and the immortal soul and the Sadducees who interpreted the scriptures in ways that rejected these beliefs.

The challenge for the ancient Israelites in their devotion to Yahweh wasn't the attraction of pagan religions but the need to leave their ancient customs to follow the prophets into a newer understanding of the nature of God. "The Baal Cycle" represents the pagan culture that ancient Israel emerged out of and against which the prophets of Yahweh reacted. (The Hebrew language has been classified by linguists as a form of the Canaanite language. Phoenician and Punic are virtually identical with Hebrew as are other Canaanite dialects such as Moabite. The language we call "Hebrew" is never called "Hebrew" in the Bible. It is described as Canaanite (Isaiah 19:18) and the Jew's language (2 Kings 18:28). Umberto Cassuto in *The Goddess Anath: Canaanite Epics on the Patriarchal Age* argued that the Baal Cycle Canaanite Epic proved that the land of Canaan in the Biblical period was a culture that produced literature and argued that this proved the antiquity of the Bible. (This means that, in a sense, the Bible is a product of the literary culture of ancient Canaan.) It is possible that while they were slaves in Egypt, the Israelites spoke a Semitic language, closely related to but distinct from the Canaanite "Hebrew" language and that they became assimilated into the Hebrew-speaking culture of Canaan in a similar manner that the Turkic Bulgars became Slavicized. The Bible describes the Israelites inter-marrying with the Canaanites during the Patriarchal period (Genesis 38:2, Exodus 6:15). According to the Bible, the Israelites failed to drive out the Canaanites. Then God decreed that they would not be driven out, but would stay in the land and be a "snare" to the Israelites (Judges 2:2-3). The Canaanites did prove to be a snare. However, some of Israel's neighbors came to follow Israel's God and united with Israel. This would include Ruth the Moabitess, the Gibeonites, Namaan the Syrian, Uriah the Hittite, Araunah the Jebusite (from whom David purchased the Temple Mount) and Achior of the Book of Judith among others. Ezekiel the Prophet even states that such gentiles shall be granted a portion of the Promised Land (Ezekiel 47:22).

In some ways, the Canaanite El is like the God we worship. El is merciful, compassionate, he is the creator of the universe and a lover of Mankind. However, we also see El in the Canaanite myths as sometimes drunken and at times licentious. The prophets had to battle against these false conceptions regarding the nature of God.

The "pagan ways" that the prophets denounced refer to the stories and the belief system found in the Baal Cycle. This is the context and not church bells, steeples, or communion as many of the false teachers who have infiltrated the "Semitic/Hebrew Roots" movement would have many believe.

I wish that everyone would find peace with God and salvation. I believe that these people in the Restorationist cults with their sick obsession with paganism, are doing great harm to the body of Christ. Almost all of the things they say about paganism are not accurate. I think they should stop posing as God's people and leave the church and focus on what it seems to me that they truly worship. They speak of Baal and Tammuz more than they do of the Sacred Scriptures. In the book of Galatians Paul says that he wishes that those who were demanding that all men who followed Jesus be circumcised would go the whole way and man cunuchs of themselves! There are now neo-pagan groups that worship the Canaanite gods. If these people are unwilling to repent, I think these Restorationist cultists should stop posing as "believers" and join these groups. That way they can indulge in their obsession with pagan gods and stop harming God's people. What Restorationist cultists are doing is just as evil and demonic as they suppose "paganism" is.

I believe that God condescended to Man. He revealed himself to the prophets in ways that they could understand through a progressive revelation.

As a Christian, I believe that the perfect revelation of God is found in Jesus Christ. Jesus offers the promise of forgiveness of sins and a better life. That is living a life of compassion and love towards our fellow human beings.

The sacrifice of the daughter of Jephthah

A Canaanite Priest

A Carthaginian Priest holding an infant

Some people dispute the claim that the Canaanites/Carthaginians engaged in human sacrifice of their children. It seems to me that the preponderance of evidence is that they did. The Greeks and Romans would often condemn the Canaanites/Carthaginians for being barbaric because they would sacrifice their own children. Some scholars believe that the claims of human sacrifice were merely propaganda directed against the Canaanites/Carthaginians. But the Bible seems to describe Canaanite and Israelite culture as engaging in human sacrifice of children. We see this in the story of Abraham and his sacrifice of Isaac and in the story of Jephthah's daughter. (According to the Bible, Abraham's sacrifice, which was not carried out, was a test of faith.)In the Book of Judges, Jephthah makes a rash vow to sacrifice unto Yahweh whatever creature he first sees when he arrives home if Yahweh grants him victory in battle. He did return home in victory and it was his daughter, to his great distress, that greeted him. She was his only child. Some Bible scholars believe that when she was "devoted to Yahweh" that this means that she was made a servant of the Tabernacle of God and in a way was forced to join a religious order. Most scholars believe that she was given in a human sacrifice. Those scholars believe this story shows the great extent in which Israelite culture had been corrupted by Canaanite practices. (As does the story of Micah in the Book of Judges. Micah worships Yahweh, but builds a silver idol out of money he had previously stolen from his mother. The idol may have been an idol of El or perhaps even Yahweh (or some other god). Micah even employed the grandson of Moses to be his personal priest. All of his idols and other cultic objects were stolen from him by the Danites, who also kidnapped Moses' grandson in order that he would be their priest! The high place of Tel-Dan was founded by them.) The Law of Moses forbids the Israelites to offer their babies as human sacrifices and the Bible and the Prophets often condemn wicked rulers and others for "passing their sons through the fire" in a human sacrifice. And there is also the story of King Mesha, a Moabite king, who sacrificed his son when the battle seemed to turn against him. (Hiel the Bethelite may have sacrificed his sons in dedication to his rebuilt city of Jericho (1 Kings 16:34). Joshua cursed the city saying that whoever would rebuild it would lose his own sons (Joshua 6:36).)Why would the Law of Moses and the Prophets of Yahweh condemn a practice that was unknown among the Canaanites and Israelites? The Greeks and Romans may have exaggerated the extent to which the practice of child sacrifice existed in Canaanite/Carthaginian society but it seems that, even if the practice was rare, it was not unknown. The drawing above shows a Carthaginian priest holding a child. Most people interpret this as the priest preparing to sacrifice the child. But he may be blessing the child or preparing a deceased child for burial. The debate on the issue and the extent of child sacrifice among the Canaanites/Carthaginians continues.

An Ancient Egyptian depiction of Canaanites

Here we see how ancient Egyptians saw the Canaanites. I think it is interesting that they are wearing tassels on the fringes of their garments. Moses mandated this practice for all Jewish men and this custom is still observed among Jews to this day (Numbers 15:38, Deuteronomy 22:12). Moses required that the tassel (Tzit-Tzit) be dyed blue with the dye from the murex sea snail.

***Hexaplex trunculus** (also known as **Murex trunculus** or the **banded dye-murex**) is a medium-sized species of sea snail, a marine gastropod mollusk in the family Muricidae, the murex shells or rock snails. This species of sea snail is important historically because its hypobranchial gland secretes a mucus that the ancient Canaanites/Phoenicians used as a distinctive purple-blue indigo dye. One of the dye's main chemical ingredients is dibromo-indigotin, and if left in the sun for a few minutes before becoming fast, its color turns to a blue indigo (like blue jeans).*

*The Old Testament mentions a specific blue dye, called **Tekhelet** for use in the Priestly garments as well in the layman's tzitzit, the formal tassels or fringes of clothing, which some believe refers to the indigo dye from the Hexaplex trunculus when kept in the sun. Similarly, the Hebrew Bible also mentions a specific purple dye, called **argaman** which refers to the purple color this same dye produces when kept in the shade.*

Tekelet "turquoise" or "blue; also techelet) is a blue dye from a shellfish called Chilazon mentioned 50 times in the Old Testament. It was used in the clothing of the High Priest, the tapestries in the Tabernacle, and the tassels affixed to the corners of one's four-cornered garments.

The ancient method for mass-producing purple-blue dye from Hexaplex trunculus has not yet been successfully reproduced (because the purplish hue degrades too quickly, resulting in blue only). Nonetheless the use of this species in dyeing "purple-blue" has been confirmed in the archeology of Phoenicia, where large quantities of the shells have been recovered from inside ancient live storage chambers that were used for harvesting. Allegedly, 10-12,000 murex were needed to produce one gram of dye. The dye was highly prized in ancient times. Sometimes known as royal blue, it was prohibitively expensive and was only used by the highest ranking aristocracy.

A similar dye, Tyrian purple, which is purple-red in color, was made from a related species of marine snail, Murex brandaris. This dye (alternatively known as imperial purple) was also prohibitively expensive.

Tyrian purple also known as royal purple, imperial purple or imperial dye, is a reddish-purple natural dye, which is a secretion produced by certain species of predatory sea snails in the family Muricidae, a type of rock snail by the name Murex. This dye was possibly first used by the ancient Phoenicians as early as 1600 BCE. The dye was greatly prized in antiquity because the colour did not easily fade, but instead became brighter with weathering and sunlight.

(Also, remember, in the story Anath appeals to Mot for mercy and grabs the "fringes" of his garment. Tzit-Tzit are also referred to in the stories of King David and Jesus. David cut King Saul's Tzit-Tzit off (1 Samuel 24:4-5). A woman with an issue of blood was healed when she touched Christ's Tzit-Tzit (Matthew 9:20).)

SANCHUNIATHON'S GENEALOGY OF THE GODS

(SIMPLIFIED)

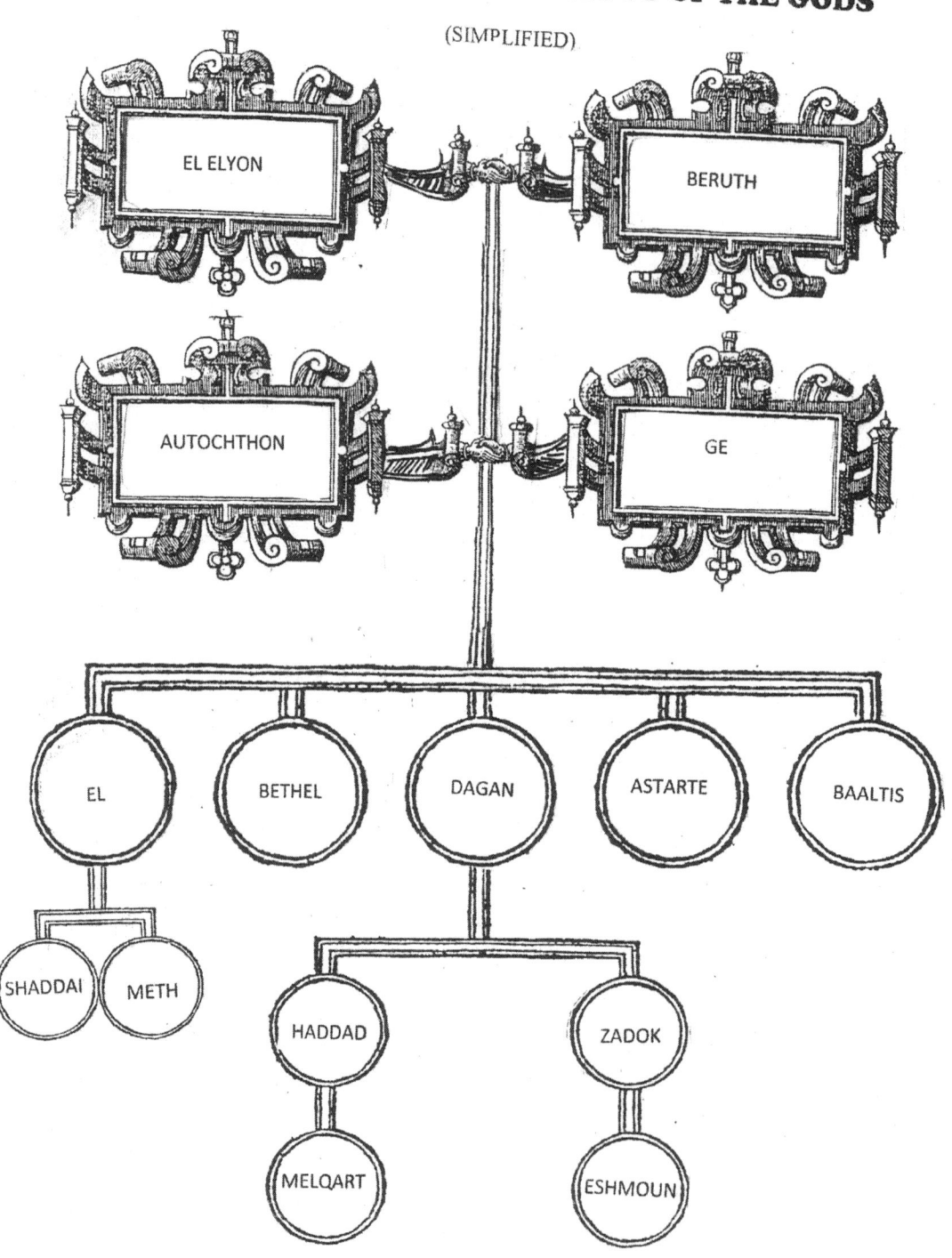

The Early Church Father Eusebius quoted from an ancient account of Canaanite mythology called "Sanchuniathon." This work is now lost except for the fragments preserved by Eusebius and others. I discuss Sanchuniathon in greater depth in the "Epic of Baal the God of Thunder." Sanchuniathon is one of the sources that I consulted in writing this book. Sanchuniathon may be an example of "Interpretatio Graeca" or the "Greek Interpretation." The Greeks would examine a foreign mythology and conform it to their own religious beliefs. They would find a God that is similar to one of their own and then say that it was the same god. For instance, since both Zeus and Baal Haddad wielded the thunderbolt, then Baal Haddad was identified as Zeus. It is likely that the ancient foreign myths were brought into conformity with the Greek religious structure. 'Interpretatio Graeca" probably in reality represented a Greek bastardization of the ancient mythology. What is interesting is that Sanchuniathon supposedly originated with a Canaanite priest of Yahweh. (This god was called "Ieuo" and may or may not have been Yahweh. We know that some Phoenicians and Syrians, such as Yahu-bidi, the King of Hammath, among others, did worship Yahweh. In the Book of Kings, King Hiram of Tyre, a Phoenician/Canaanite King recognized Yahweh as God and helps Solomon build a temple to Yahweh.) This is a simplified family tree of the Canaanite gods according to Sanchuniathon. It is interesting that the Canaanites used names the Bible uses for God in their pantheon. This includes El, Shaddai (probably meaning "Mountain" or "Almighty"), El Elyon, Bethel and Zadok. Sanchuniathon is fragmentary and it is unknown if it accurately reflects Canaanite religious beliefs or not. Of course, Eusebius quoted from it in order to disparage the Canaanite religion.

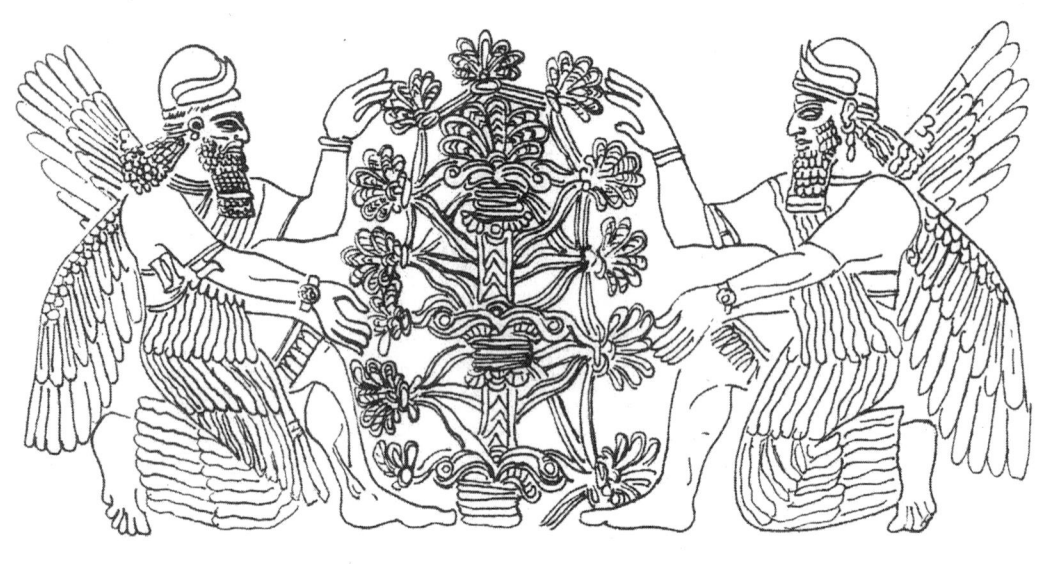

Mesopotamian depictions of the Tree of Life

Here we see a picture of a stylized "tree of life" being guarded by Mesopotamian angelic beings. This tree of life symbolism is probably similar to the Asherah tree of life "Asherah poles." The "Tree of Life" seems to be a universal symbol. In Norse mythology the Universe is viewed as a massive Tree of Life called Yggdrasil. A connection between the ancient Germanic peoples and the Semites with their "Tree of Life" is unlikely. However, some believe that Phoenician traders did have some contact with ancient Germans. Theo Vennemann thought that there was a Semitic influence upon the early Germanic peoples as can be seen in the ablaut system and in some cultural influences, such as the similarities he sees between Friyya/Frigga and Ashtoreth/Astarte/Ishtar. These theories are disputed and haven't been widely accepted in the scholarly community. However, students of Norse mythology supposed that the Germanic Dwarves of Norse Mythology may have been based upon German encounters with Phoenician and Carthaginian traders. The dwarves of mythology are miners and craftsmen. Strabo states that there was a highly lucrative Phoenician trade with Britain for tin. It was once thought that this was direct trade but it is now believed to have been indirect. Scholars previously believed that the Phoenicians mined in England. It is probably this reason that J.R.R. Tolkien used Hebrew as a basis of his Dwarvish language, which he called Khuzdul. Hebrew, Phoenician, and Punic, the Carthaginian language, are all closely related languages that linguists classify as Canaanite. I don't think that much should be made of it but it is possible that there may have been some limited contact between the early proto-Germanic peoples and Phoenicians, but it should be remembered that Germanic peoples are Indo-Europeans and are not Semitic.

A Xoanon

This is an ancient stone copy of a xoanon. The "Asherah poles" mentioned in the Bible were most likely very similar to a xoanon. We see that it is a log that has a few crude sculptings upon it. Asherah poles were similar crudely carved totem poles.

The Omphalos Stone

This is the Baetylus Stone of Delphi in Greece. The use of these small sacred stone idols were common in the ancient world. Similar sacred stones are used in Hinduism. These Hindu Baetylus Stones called "Shivalinga" are depicted in the "Indiana Jones and the Temple of Doom" movie. In the Bible at the story of "Jacob's ladder" is a reference to the Baetylus of Bethel. (Baetylus is simply the Greek way of saying "Bethel.") The Baetylus was small enough for Jacob to use as a pillow.

An ancient coin showing an image of the Elagabalus Baetylus of Emesa in Syria

This was viewed as the Sacred Stone of El Gabal-a name of El likely equivalent to the name El Shaddai. When we think of ancient idols, we shouldn't necessary think of all idols as being sculptures. Plain stones, meteorites and oddly shaped stones were also used as idols. We have seen this with the xoanon. Two Roman Emperors tried to elevate El Gabalus, as they called El, as the one supreme god of the Roman Empire. Constantine was finally able to establish monotheism over the Roman Empire.

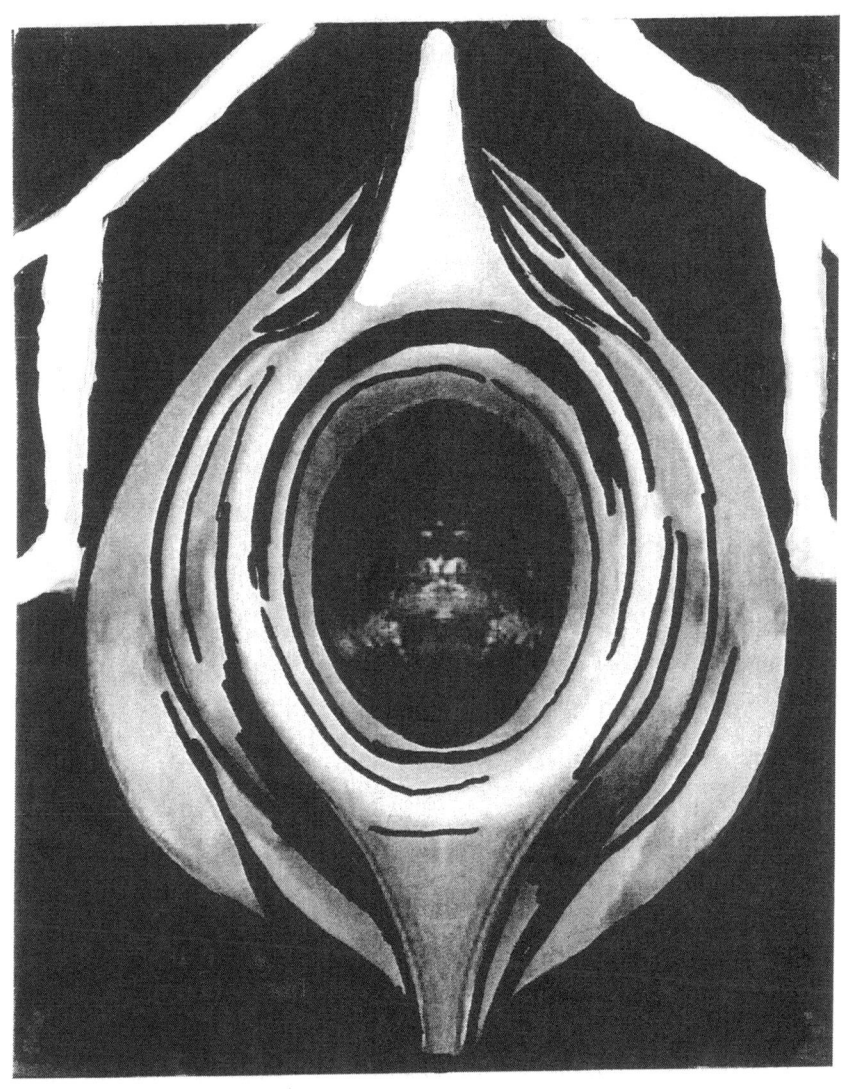

The Black Stone Baetylus of Mecca

Islam still venerates a Baetylus Stone. The Black Stone is the only idol that Mohammed spared when he took over Mecca. This wasn't the first time that he tried to accommodate pagans by incorporating their idolatry and polytheism into his new religion. For a time he allowed Muslims to worship the "Three Daughters of Allah" as will be discussed below. I discuss the issues of Baetyli and the Black Stone of Mecca in "The Epic of Baal the God of Thunder." Muslims are required to attempt to touch the "Black Stone" during their Hajj ceremonies. We know from ancient accounts that other pre-Islamic pagan Arab sanctuaries had Baetyli similar to the Black Stone of Mecca.

The Goddesses of Islam-these are the three goddesses Mohammed allowed his followers to worship

During the infamous "Satanic Verses" incident, Mohammed allowed Moslems to worship the "Three Goddesses of Islam" for a period of time. In fact, the Koran contained a sura sanctioning the intercession of the "Daughters of Allah." The Daughters of Allah were Allat-equivalent to Asherah, Al-Uzza, equivalent to Ashtoreth, and Al-Manat, equivalent to Sheol. Islam means submission and Mohammed used this sura as an attempt to get the Meccans to submit to his rule. When Mohammed realized that this tactic wasn't bringing about the results which he desired, he claimed that the devil tricked him and he revised the sura to take out the verse allowing Muslims to pray to the daughters of Allah. I discuss this more in depth in the "Epic of Baal."

In the drawing, note the sacred tree and the guardian cat. The sacred tree is similar to an Asherah Sacred Grove and the guardian cat is similar to Ariel, the lion that guards Ashtoreth in this story. The veneration of sacred trees was an ancient Semitic practice. The radical Wahibi cult of Saudi Arabia that originated in the 1700s would repress the veneration of sacred trees by desert Arabs in its early days. (Unfortunately, this dangerous cult is still active in the world today.) The cat is a caracal. To my delight, I saw one of these magnificent animals in the wild when I was on guard duty in the rural suburbs in the extremity of Baghdad.

In my drawing, first we see Al-lat, the goddess and the Arabian equivalent of Asherah. Her name means "the Goddess" and is a feminine form of Allah. She was called the mother of the gods. Al-Lat seems to be often confused or sometimes identified with Al-Uzza. This was also true of Asherah and Ashtoreth who were often confused with or identified with each other. She is holding a sheaf of wheat at the top of which is the Sun, since she may have been a goddess of the Sun. On her necklace she wears a crescent moon, which was one of her symbols.

Al-Uzza means "the Strong One." She is the Arabian equivalent of Ashtoreth, but she has a martial aspect, similar to Anath. The church father Isaac of Antioch calls Her Beltis ("Lady", a title shared by many other Semitic Goddesses), and Kaukabta, "the Star".

Manat or Manawayat derives her name from Arabic maniya, "fate, destruction, doom, death", or menata, "part, portion, that which is alloted". She is a Goddess of Death, and Maniya (Death personified) and in this picture she is holding out the cup of death.

It should be noted that Arab women had extensive rights in Arab culture before the dawn of Islam. Zenobia was a powerful Arabian queen who challenged the might of Rome. After the death of Mohammed, many Arab women celebrated his death and led Arabian armies in resistance to Islam. In my opinion, it is unfortunate that the woman led "War of Apostasy" against Islam was unsuccessful and I admire those heroic Arab women who fought and died in resistance to Islam. Moslems call the pre-Islamic period the Age of Jahiliya-meaning the period of darkness. I view the pre-Islamic Arabian view of the status of women as more enlightened than that held by many Moslems today. I have traveled all across the Middle East and my heart broke at the inhumanity in how women are often treated in the Islamic world. The cruelty is widespread because I saw it in the different countries I visited. I do love the Middle East and its peoples. Arabs are a kind people, but I am outraged at the way I saw Coptic Christians, Assyrian Christians and women being treated in the Middle East.

Thalia Took has written an excellent article on "The Arab Triple Goddess" which I recommend. Her website on ancient goddesses is very helpful.

The Elohim (gods) and Baalim (lords) 0f
Canaanite Mythology

Glossary of the Canaanite Gods and Goddesses

This book is not intended to be an exhaustive treatment about all the Canaanite gods nor was it my chief concern in writing this story to be as accurate as possible. It seems to me that scholarly consensus is still being worked out. There seems to be different opinions and interpretations of the texts. In fact, my main concern in writing the story was narrative flow and to tell the basic story and not to create a comprehensive and authoritative account. If a god or goddess didn't serve that end, I left them out of my version of the Baal Cycle. This story is a product of my imagination. However, almost all of what I wrote is derived from the Ugaritic texts, the Bible, Greek versions of Canaanite myths and other ancient sources. More in depth information can be found in the books listed in the references section. In the story I had to fill in the gaps using my imagination where our knowledge is fragmentary. Scholars do disagree in some of the interpretations of these ancient texts and these issues are discussed academically in several helpful books that are listed below. At times, I restructured the myths in order to create a coherent narrative. I want to be accurate but I was also motivated by the desire to make these ancient stories more accessible to a modern audience. But, on the other hand, there is ongoing debate about the structure of these myths.

In the Bible, Elohim usually means God. It is a plural noun and is used to denote "gods" in certain passages of Scripture. In Ugarit, the word "Elohim" is used to mean "the gods" and refers to all of their gods. The God of the Bible is often called El. But, it seems that the El of the Bible is not the same God as the El that the Canaanites worshiped. Or at least that is how the prophets and the writers of the Bible viewed it. The Israelite people had different opinions and obviously some of them did view their El as the same god worshiped by their Canaanite neighbors. By the way, linguists classify Hebrew as a Canaanite dialect and the writers of the Bible never call their language Hebrew. They called the language they spoke and wrote the Bible in "Canaanite" and "the Judean language." (See above.)

Ambrosian Stones: According to Nonnus (late 4th or early 5th century) in his epic poem *Dionysiaca* in which he tells the story of the god Dionysus and his journey to India and triumphal return, Melqart tells Dionysus how he taught the primeval, earthborn inhabitants of Phoenicia how to build the first boat and instructed them to sail out to a pair of floating, rocky islands. On one of the islands there grew an olive tree with a serpent at its foot, an eagle at its summit, and which glowed in the middle with fire that burned but did not consume. Following the god's instructions, these primeval humans sacrificed the eagle to Poseidon [Yam], Zeus [Baal Haddad], and the other gods. Thereupon the islands rooted themselves to the bottom of the sea. On these islands the city of Tyre was founded. The story is found in the 40th book of the *Dionysiaca*. In this version of the Baal story, I have the "Ambrosian Stone" as a manifestation of the goddess Asherah.

Anath: Goddess of war and sexuality. Anath is mentioned in the Holy Bible. The daughter of El, Anath is the sister and lover of Baal. Anath was worshiped with Yahweh (called Yahu) in Elephantine in Egypt by the Judean settlers there. These Judeans apparently viewed Anath as the wife of Jehovah. Anath is mentioned in the Bible in Judges 3:31 and 5:6 and in the book of Jeremiah, Anath is also mentioned in toponyms in Beth Anath in Naphtali (Joshua 1:33) and Beth-Anath in Judah (Joshua 15:59) and Anathoth, north of Jerusalem (Jeremiah 1:1). Anath was worshiped by the Syrians who settled in Egypt and by the Egyptians. Cassuto describes Anath in his book as a "goddess distinguished for her heroic spirit and courage. She is a mighty fighter, who devastates her foes and loves to bathe her feet in the blood of those she has slain. She is a loyal sister to Baal, supports him in his struggle against Mot, inflicts terrible blows upon the confederates of Mot, and when Mot succeeds in slaying Baal, she avenges him with unrestrained fury." (Page 64). Some scholars believe that Anath is strictly a goddess of war and claim that there is no evidence that she was a goddess of love or sex.

Annakin: A race of brutes that was created to serve the gods but who later rebelled. The **Anunnaki** (also transcribed as: **Anunna, Anunnaku, Ananaki** and other variations) are a group of deities in ancient Mesopotamian cultures (i.e., Sumerian, Akkadian, Assyrian and Babylonian). The Annakim are lesser deities that were created to perform labor at the behest of the gods. The name is variously written "a-nuna", "a-nuna-ke-ne", or "a-nun-na", meaning something to the effect of "those of royal blood" or 'princely offspring'. Their relation to the group of gods known as the Igigi is unclear — at times the names are used synonymously but in the Atra-Hasis flood myth the Igigi have to work for the Anunnaki, rebelling after 40 days and replaced by the creation of humans. In the Bible there are the sons of Anak, called the Anakim, who are described as being a race of giants and as being Nephilim (Numbers 13:33, Joshua 15:13). The Bible describes the Anakites as Rephaim in (Deuteronomy 2:11). Anunnaki (Anunna) perhaps means "great gods" in Mesopotamian myth. Some have argued that it could perhaps mean sons of the god Anu, the gods of the heavens and the king of gods, spirits and demons. The seven judges of hell are called the Annunaki, the descendents of Lahamu and Lahmu-the "muddy ones."Anunnaki was used of the great gods of heaven collectively and was later used to refer to the gods of the underworld.

Ariel: The Lion of El. (Arya-El in Canaanite.) The protector of Ashtoreth.

Arsay: A "woman of Baal," either his wife or daughter or perhaps both. Her name has been translated as "maid of floods" in the past, but now it is often translated as "earth-maiden." Her name may indicate a relationship with Baal due to his time under the earth in the netherworld.

Asherah: She is called Athirat. Mother goddess and sacred tree. She is Elat-the goddess. In this re-telling of the story, I decided to portray her as like a wood nymph (a Dryad/Hamadryad) in Greek mythology. I also decided to make the tree on the Ambrosian Stones in the Melqart myth into Asherah. She is also the Lady of Byblos (Balaat Gebel). Asherah is also called Lady Asherah of the Sea. In the Epic of Gilgamesh we see the Tree of Life beneath the waters of the sea. Gilgamesh swims under the water and takes the fruit. However, it is stolen from him by a serpent, when he rests from this endeavor. Some scholars believe the Asherah and Ashtoreth, which were originally two distinct goddesses, became compounded together as one goddess during the Old Testament period. However, the biblical Ashtoreth should not be confused with the goddess Asherah, the form of the names being quite distinct, and both appearing quite distinctly in the Book of 1st Kings.

Asherah Pole: (See Xoanon) An **Asherah pole** is a sacred tree or pole that stood near Canaanite religious locations to honor the Canaanite mother-goddess Asherah, the wife of El. The relation of the literary references to an *asherah* and archaeological finds of Judaean pillar-figurines has engendered a literature of debate. The Hebrew Bible suggests that the poles were made of wood. In the sixth chapter of the Book of Judges, God is recorded as instructing the Israelite judge Gideon to cut down an Asherah pole that was next to an altar to Baal. The wood was to be used for a burnt offering. Deuteronomy 16:21 states that YHWH (rendered as "the LORD") hated *Asherim* whether rendered as poles: "Do not set up any [*wooden*] Asherah [*pole*] beside the altar you build to the LORD your God" or as living trees: "You shall not plant any tree as an Asherah beside the altar of the Lord your God which you shall make". However, the record indicates that the Jewish people often departed from this ideal. For example, King Manasseh placed an Asherah pole in the Holy Temple (2 Kings 21:7). King Josiah's reforms in the late 7th century BC included the destruction of many Asherah poles (2 Kings 23). That Asherahs were not always living trees is shown in 1 Kings 14:23: "their asherim, beside every luxuriant tree". Exodus 34:13 states: "Break down their altars, smash their sacred stones and cut down their Asherah poles." Some biblical archaeologists have suggested that until the 6th century BC the Israelite peoples had household shrines, or at least figurines, of Asherah, which are strikingly common in the archaeological remains. Many of these statuettes of the naked goddess holding up her breasts with her hands have been discovered.

Ashtoreth: Also called Astarte, Ishtar and Athtart. Ashtoreth is the goddess of sex and sensuality. She is the Morning star. The Sumerians called Isthtar Inanna. Inanna was associated with the celestial planet, Venus. There are hymns to Inanna as her astral manifestation. It also is believed that in many myths about Inanna, including *Inanna's Descent to the Underworld* and *Inanna and Shukaletuda*, her movements correspond with the movements of Venus in the sky. Also, because of its positioning so close to Earth, Venus moves rather irregularly across the sky, and never travels all the way across the dome of the sky as most celestial bodies do, instead, Venus rises in the East and the West in both the morning and evening. Because of Venus's erratic movements (it disappears behind the sun from 90–3 days at a time and then reappears on the other horizon), some cultures did not recognize Venus as single entity, but rather two separate stars on each horizon as the morning and evening star. The Mesopotamians, however, most likely understood that the planet was one entity. A Cylinder seal from the *Jemdet Nasr* Period expresses the knowledge that both morning and evening stars were the same celestial entity. The erratic movements of Venus relate to both mythology as well as Inanna's erratic nature. Like Venus, Inanna seems unpredictable in her actions, being both the goddess of love and war, having both masculine and feminine qualities, and occasionally having temper tantrums.

Mesopotamian literature, however, takes this comparison one step further, explaining Inanna's physical movements in mythology as similar to the movements of Venus in the sky. *Inanna's Descent to the Underworld* explains how Inanna is able to, unlike any other deity, descend into the netherworld and return to the heavens. The planet Venus appears to make a similar descent, setting in the West and then rising again in the East. In *Inanna and Shukaletuda*, in search of her attacker, Inanna makes several movements throughout the myth that correspond with the movements of Venus in the sky. An introductory hymn explains Inanna leaving the heavens and heading for *Kur*, what could be presumed to be, the mountains, replicating the rising and setting of Inanna to the West. Shukaletuda also is described as scanning the heavens in search of Inanna, possibly to the eastern and western horizons. Inanna was associated with the eastern fish of the last of the zodiacal constellations, Pisces. Her consort Dumuzi was associated with the contiguous first constellation, Aries. Some scholars believe that after several centuries of being worshiped as two distinct goddesses, Asherah and Ashtoreth were eventually merged together in the minds of their adherents as a single goddess. However, the biblical Ashtoreth should not be confused with the goddess Asherah, the form of the names being quite distinct, and both appearing quite distinctly in the Book of 1st Kings.

Atargatis or **Ataratheh** (Aramaic: *'Atar'atheh* or *Tar'atheh*) was a Syrian deity, the chief goddess of northern Syria. Commonly known to the ancient Greeks by the name **Aphrodite Derceto** and to the Romans as *Dea Syriae* ("Goddess of Syria"), occasionally rendered in one word **Deasura**. She was most likely a form of Ashtoreth. Her chief sanctuary was at Hierapolis, modern Manbij, northeast of Aleppo, Syria. She is often now popularly described as the mermaid-goddess, from her fish-bodied appearance at Ashkelon. In the temples of Atargatis at Palmyra and at Dura-Europos she appeared repeatedly with her consort, Hadad, and in the richly syncretic religious culture at Dura-Europos, was worshipped as *Artemis Azzanathkona*. According to a third-century Syriac source, "In Syria and in Urhâi [Edessa] the men used to castrate themselves in honor of Taratha. But when King Abgar became a Christian, he commanded that anyone who emasculated himself should have a hand cut off." This successfully abolished the practice.

Athtar: A god of war. Athtar seems to be a male form of Ishtar/Ashtoreth. Both Ishtar and Athtar descend into hell. This is because of astrological reasons described above. Both Athtar and Ashtoreth are the Morning Star/the planet Venus. The story of Athtar and Sheol in this book is based on the story of Nergal and Ereshkigal. Nergal is mentioned in the Bible at 2 Kings 17:30. Some scholars believe that certain texts in the Bible thought to refer to the fall of Lucifer are actually alluding to myths about the fall of Athtar.

Baal: A title meaning "lord" that could refer to many different gods. Most often refers to Haddad, the god of thunder. He was called Adad in Akkadian, the language of Assyria and Babylonia. He was also called Rimmon, Aramaic for "the Thunderer." Baal sustains life and is a god of life and the embodiment of forces that give, preserve and renew life.

Baetylus (also **Bethel**, or **Betyl**) is a word denoting a sacred stone, which was supposedly endowed with life. According to ancient sources, these objects of worship were meteorites, which were dedicated to the gods or revered as symbols of the gods themselves. An example is also mentioned at Bethel in Genesis 28:11-19. In the Phoenician mythology related by Sanchuniathon, one of the sons of Uranus was named *Baetylus*. The worship of baetyli was widespread in the Phoenician colonies, including Carthage, even after the adoption of Christianity, and was denounced by St. Augustine of Hippo. In ancient Greek religion and myth, the term was specially applied to the Omphalos, the stone supposed to have been swallowed by Cronus (who feared misfortune from his own children) in mistake for his infant son Zeus, for whom it had been substituted by Gaea. This stone was carefully preserved at Delphi, anointed with oil every day and on festive occasions covered with raw wool. (In the Scriptural citation from Genesis, Jacob put a small stone under his head and used it for a pillow. He had a spiritual experience. The next morning, he erected the stone upon a shrine and anointed it with oil and declared the place a Bethel-which means in Hebrew-"House of EL.") In Rome, there was the stone effigy of Rhea Cybele, or Mater Idaea Deum, that had been ceremoniously brought from Pessinus in Asia Minor in 204 BCE. Another conical meteorite was enshrined in the Elagabalium to personify Elagabalus Sol Invictus. Often, baetyli were rather plain stones. In some cases an attempt was made to give a more regular form to the original shapeless stone: thus Apollo Agyieus was represented by a conical pillar with pointed end, Zeus Meilicirius in the form of a pyramid. Other famous baetylic idols were those in the temples of Zeus Casius at Seleucia Pieria, and of Zeus Teleios at Tegea. Even in the declining years of paganism, these idols still retained their significance, as is shown by the attacks upon them by ecclesiastical writers. Among monotheists, the practice survives today with Islam's Black Stone. Muslims face their Black Stone Baetylus in prayer five times a day. When hey perform the Hajj, their pilgrimage ritual, they are to try to touch the Baetylus. If they can't touch the Black Stone, they must reach towards it or point at it. I discuss this issue more in depth in "The Epic of Baal the God of Thunder." It is interesting that, according to the Book of Judges, the Ark of the Covenant was kept at the city of Bethel for a time during the Benjamite War. It is also interesting that the Israelites consulted the Lord at Bethel during the War with the Tribe of Benjamin. The Bible isn't clear how they consulted the Lord. Did they consult the Beatylus, the Ephod, or the Ark of the Covenant? Or did the High Priest Phineas serve as a prophet and speak the word of the Lord? The Bible isn't clear on this issue. It seems that before the time of David, the Ark of the Covenant was kept at Shiloh. (Until the Philistines destroyed the sanctuary at Shiloh.)

Behemoth: A chaos monster of earth.

Cherubim: Winged sphinxes that guard the gods. They are the guardians of El and of the Garden of Eden.

Dagon: The god of grain. Incorrectly identified by rabbis who knew nothing of Canaanite mythology as a fish god. Dagan or Dagon (two pronunciations of the same god) is described as being the father of Baal. Probably known as Baal Hammon.

El: "God." Ēl is the grey-bearded ancient one, full of wisdom, the kindly and compassionate one. Ēl is called again and again *Tôru ʿĒl* ("Bull Ēl" or "the bull god"). He is *bātnyu binwāti* ("Creator of creatures"), *ʾabū banī ʾili* ("father of the gods"), and *ʿabū ʿadami* ("father of man"). He is *qāniyunu ‘ôlam* ("creator eternal"), the epithet *ôlam* appearing in Hebrew form in the Hebrew name of God *’ēl ‘ôlam* "God Eternal" in Genesis 21.33. He is *hātikuka* ("your patriarch").El is called *malku* ("king"), *’abū šamīma* ("father of years"), and *’ēl gibbōr* ("Ēl the warrior"). There was a temple to Baal Hadad and to Dagon that have been discovered at Ugarit but no temple of El has been discovered there yet. However, this may have been because the holy sanctuary of El was a tabernacle or a tent. Some have postulated that perhaps El was the same god as Dagan as being the reason that there is no temple of El at Ugarit. Other scholars dispute this theory.

Elohim: Literally "gods." In the Ugaritic texts "Elohim" means gods and is used in reference to all the gods. In the Holy Bible, the word "Elohim" is used to refer to the God of Israel.

Eshmoun: God of healing. A great God of Sidon. Son of Tsaddick (or Zadok). Photius in *Bibliotheca* Codex 242 summarizes Damascius as saying that Asclepius of Beirut (Asclepius was the Greek god of medicine so here we have another example of *Interpretatio Graeca*) was a youth who was fond of hunting. He was seen by the goddess Astronoë (thought by many scholars to be a version of Ashtoreth) who so harassed him with amorous pursuit that in desperation he castrated himself and died. Astronoë then named the youth *Paeon* 'Healer', restored him to life from the warmth of her body, and changed him into a god. A village near Beirut named Qabr Shmoun, "Eshmoun's grave," still exists.

Gupin-wa-Ugar: This name means "Vine and Cultivated Field" and belongs to a servant of Baal.

Horon: (also spelled Hauron) A son of Ashtoreth and a god of the wilderness, of warriors and of the netherworld.

Leviathan: A chaos monster of the waters.

Lilith: A night demon in Jewish myth. Some scholars have argued that a Babylonian background exists for Lilith. In Akkadian Lilitu. Lilu means "spirit" in Akkadian. In Mesopotamia mythology, Lamashtu is an evil goddess expelled from heaven who pursued the human race causing disease, death of infants and discontent in family life. In Jewish myth, she was Adam's first wife, who was created as his equal, and yet left him because she refused to submit to him as his wife. She hates the descendents of Adam and kills babies in the crib. Some people believe the demon Lilith is referenced to as the "night owl" in Isaiah 34:14. These ideas are disputed. In this story, I am trying to give the Canaanite perspective. El is the father fo the gods, he begets them and then assigns to the gods and goddesses their domains. So, El fathers Shamash, the sun, Yerikh, the moon and Lilith the night and so on.

Nehustan: The serpent. The word "Nahash" is an old Canaanite word for snake. The word Nehustan is used in the Bible to describe the bronze snake that Moses made and is sometimes translated as "brass thing." The snake, and the snake on a pole, was in ancient times, and is still today, used as a symbol of healing or of the healing/medical profession.

Nephilim: The Nephilim are demigods, half-man, half-god creatures. They are described in the Bible as the offspring of the "Sons of God and the Daughters of Men." (Genesis 6:1-4).

Nikkal: Nikkal is the Canaanite Goddess of Fruits and Fertility, who is a Goddess of Orchards. Her husband is the Moon-God Yarikh, who causes the dew to fall each night and water her trees so that they may thrive. The oldest complete annotated piece of ancient music is a Hurrian song dedicated to Nikkal, a hymn in Ugaritic cuneiform syllabic writing. This was published upon its discovery in Ugarit by Emmanuel Laroche, first in 1955 and then more fully in 1968, and has been the focus of many subsequent studies in palaeomusicology by, amongst others, Anne Draffkorn Kilmer, who gave it the title of "The Hymn to Nikkal."

Meth: The God of death. Meth, Mot, or Muth, means "death." We find names with the word "Mot" in them that some scholars see as Mot-compound names. This includes Methuselah, the longest living man in Genesis, and Methushael. (Meth-uselah possibly meaning "his death shall bring judgment" or "Meth shall bring judgment" Genesis 5:21-27. Meth-ushael is of uncertain meaning and is found in Genesis 4:18.) In Akkadian, Mot is used to refer to men probably an equivalent to the word "mortal," which is used for human beings in English and also means "to die," which is an important aspect of our humanity in this realm. Another Mot-compound name is found in the Bible. This is Azmaweth, or Azmaveth, which means, "Mot is Mighty." This personal name is found in 2 Samuel 23:31, 1 Chronicles 8:36, 9:42, 11:33, 12:3, 27:25. The place-name "Beth-Azmaweth" is mentioned in Ezra 2:24 and Nehemiah 7:28, 12:29. Sanchuniathon says that of the waters of chaos "Mot was produced, which some say is mud, and others a putrescence of watery compound; and out of this came every germ of creation, and the generation of the universe. So there were certain animals which had no sensation, and out of them grew intelligent animals, and were called "Zophasemin," that is "observers of heaven"; and they were formed like the shape of an egg. Also Mot burst forth into light, and sun, and moon, and stars, and the great constellations." The language here is confusing, a bad summary and possibly corrupt, and the form *Mot* here is not the same as *Muth* which appears later in the Greek and in the later section in the Greek, Muth is clearly identified with Death. But it may be that the full and coherent account would have made clear that muddy and putrescent Death is the source of life. In our world, as it exists now, there is a connection between life and death in earth's biological system. In the Canaanite myths of Ugarit, Mot is a destroyer and isn't a creator of life. The prophet condemns the Judeans for making a covenant with Death (Mot) and an agreement with Hell (Sheol) in Isaiah 28:15-18.

Molech: (also Milcom) This was the god worshiped by the Ammonites. Milcom may refer to the souls of past kings that were worshiped.

Pidray: Pidray is the maid of light. Her name probably means "misty" or "cloudy" and shows a connection with Baal who is the giver of rain. She is a "woman" (meaning a wife or daughter or perhaps both) of Baal.

Ptah: Ptah is the god of construction, metalworking, and sculpture. He was also the patron god of carpenters and shipbuilders in general. He gave his name to Egypt. (The PT in Egypt is from the name Ptah.) The English name *Egypt* derives from an ancient Egyptian name for Memphis,

Hikuptah, which means "Home of the Soul of Ptah". This entered Ancient Greek as *Aiguptos*, which entered Latin as *Ægyptus*, which developed into English as *Egypt*. In some Egyptian myths, Ptah is the Creator-god, who spoke the Universe into existence as Elohim is portrayed as doing in Genesis 1. He was called *Ptah lord of truth, Ptah master of justice, Ptah who listens to prayers, Ptah master of ceremonies,* and *Ptah lord of eternity.* The Canaanites called Ptah, *Kothar-wa-Khasis*, which means skillful and wise, and perhaps Elisha. Ptah is the creator god par excellence: He is considered the demiurge who existed before all things, and by his willingness, *thought* the world into existence. It was first conceived by Thought, and realized by the Word: *Ptah conceives the world by the thought of his heart and gives life through the magic of his Word.* That which Ptah commanded was created, with which the constituents of nature, fauna, and flora, are contained. He also plays a role in the preservation of the world and the permanence of the royal function. Ptah is generally represented in the guise of a man with green skin, contained in a shroud sticking to the skin, wearing the divine beard, and holding a scepter combining three powerful symbols of Egyptian mythology: the *Was* scepter, the sign of life, *Ankh* and the *Djed* pillar. These three combined symbols indicate the three creative powers of the god: power (the *was*), life (*ankh*) and stability (*djed*). In this story Kothar-wa-Khasis is Elisha, which is what the scholars originally thought. But now, Elisha is seen as the "herald god" and perhaps a distinct god. In this story I have expanded the role of Ptah. (I wanted to include him in the Ennead story but I thought that by doing so, it wouldn't portray the story as the people of Heliopolis believed it. I did mention Ptah in the Ennead commentary.) In this story, Kothar-wa-khasis is Elisha the herald god, although some scholars now view them as different gods. Kothar and Elisha as the same character helped me stream-line the story and emphasize a character I liked. Some scholars believe Elisha (or Ilisha) to mean "Cyrus." In the Bible Elisha is one of the greatest prophets. The name Elisha means "My God (El) is Salvation."

Qodesh-wa-Amrur: This name means "Holy and Blessed" and belongs to a servant of Baal.

Rahab: The chaos monster defeated by God at creation. The story of the battle between God and Rahab is mentioned in the Holy Bible at Job 9:13, 26:12, Psalm 89:10and Isaiah 51:9. (Rahab is mentioned in these verses in the Hebrew. If your English version mentions Rahab or not depends on how accurately the translation you are using reflects the original Hebrew text.)

Rephaim: The Rephaim are the immortal souls of departed spirits. The Rephaim, the Spirits of the Dead, rest in Sheol but the glorified dead can interact with the world of the living. Rephaim are the residents of the Netherworld (in the Hebrew Bible - **Sheol**). They are the departed spirits of human beings. In the Bible, possible examples of this usage are Isa. 14:9, 26:14,19; Ps. 88:11; Prov. 2:18, 9:18, 21:16; Job. 26:5; and possibly 2Chron. 16:12, where we may read "Repha'im," i.e. "dead ancestors," as opposed to Rophe'im, "doctors." Heb. Root Rapha means "heal," and thus the masc. plural nominalized form of this root may indicate that these **deceased ancestors** could be invoked for ritual purposes that would benefit the living. Ugaritic texts important evidence for understanding Ugarit's cult of the dead, wherein beings called *rapi'uma*, the long dead, and *malakuma*, recently dead kings, were invoked in a funeral liturgy, presented with food/drink offerings, and asked to provide blessings for the reign of the current king. (See Molech and Milcom above.) The many references to *repha'im* in the Hebrew Bible in contexts involving Sheol and dead spirits strongly suggests that many ancient Israelites imagined the spirits of the dead as playing an active and important role in securing blessings, healing, or other benefits in the lives of the living. The Bible and archeological discoveries show that the Israelites did believe in the immortality of the soul. The reason that the issue of the afterlife seems vague in the Old Testament is because it was de-emphasized because the authors of the Bible wanted to encourage worship of Yahweh alone and discourage ancestor worship, which was widely practiced. There are many who misunderstand the Bible on this issue and incorrectly think that the Israelites did not believe in the immortality of the soul.

Resheph: A god of pestilence. An attendant of Yahweh in Habakkuk 3:5.

Saphon: (or Zaphon) The Holy Mountain of the Gods. Called Mount Casius by the Greeks. (This Greek word is probably derived from the Canaanite/Hebrew word "Kassi" which means "Seat" as in "Seat of the Gods." It is modern day Mount (Jebel in Arabic) Aqraa. The Bible speaks of Mount Zaphon (which is occasionally translated in the King James as "sides of the north) in Psalm 48:1-2 and Isaiah 14:13.

Seraphim: Winged serpents that serve as the guardians of the gods.

Shalim: The god of dusk. The evening star.

Shachar: (or Shahar) Shachar is the god of dawn in the pantheon of Ugarit. He is the twin brother and counterpart of Shalim, the god of dusk. The name is a cognate of the Hebrew word *Shahar* meaning *dawn*.

Shamash: The god of the sun and of justice. Later, there was a tendency among the Greeks and the Romans to identify the sun-god as the high god. In ancient times, the sun was an important deity but was not always indentified with the high god.

Shapash: A female version of Shamash that was worshiped in the Canaanite city of Ugarit.

Sheol: In this version of the Epic of Baal she is the goddess of the Netherworld. The term in Hebrew means a grave or pit, was the place where the dead gathered, as thought by the early Hebrews, and was believed located beneath the earth, perhaps at the roots of mountains. The dead were thought to lead a conscious shadowy existence there, they were not in torment, but had neither hope nor satisfaction. Some thought they remained cut off from God. Sheol was seen as being beneath the earth, where the dead go to, a place of the gathering of the dead. People went sorrowfully to Sheol and it contained sorrows; therefore, it was viewed as gloomy. It was thought both the good and evil went there. According to the Scriptures, God's rulership over it is recognized (Amos ix. 2; Hos. xiii. 14; Deut. xxxii. 22; I Sam. ii. 6 [Isa. vii. 11]; Prov. xv. 11). God has the power to save the just in Sheol (Ps. xvi. 10).

Sheol is spoken of as a land (Job x. 21, 22); but ordinarily it is a place with gates (*ib.* xvii. 16, xxxviii. 17; Isa. xxxviii. 10; Ps. ix. 14), and seems to have been viewed as divided into compartments (Prov. vii. 27), with "farthest corners" (Isa. xiv. 15; Ezek. xxxii. 23, Hebr.; R. V. "uttermost parts of the pit"), one beneath the other, Here the dead meet (Ezek. xxxii.; Isa. xiv.; Job xxx. 23) without distinction of rank or condition—the rich and the poor, the pious and the wicked, the old and the young, the master and the slave—if the description in Job iii. refers, as most likely it does, to Sheol. The dead continue after a fashion their earthly life. Jacob would mourn there (Gen. xxxvii. 35, xlii. 38); David abides there in peace (I Kings ii. 6).

In this story the character of Sheol is based largely upon Ereshkigal and the Aramaic goddess Shuwala. Rachel S. Hallote says, in her book "Death, Burial, and the Afterlife in the Biblical World," "Shuwala is a goddess of death mentioned in texts from a city called Emar, along the Euphrates River. These ritual texts clearly identify Shuwala as the Syrian variant of Ereshkigal, Mesopotamian queen of the Netherworld. Shuwala is cognate with She'ol-the underworld of the Hebrew Bible. In fact, She'ol is a feminine noun in Hebrew, most likely reflecting its origins as a name of a female goddess of death had become the place she rules, She'ol." (page 113-114).

Tallay: Her name means "dewey" and is called the maiden of rain. She is related to Baal as a deity of precipitation. She is either a wife or a daughter of Baal or perhaps both. In Greek mythology, she is Thalia, one of the "Three Graces," who were probably carried over from the Canaanite myth of the Three Daughters of Baal-Arsay, Pidray and Tallay.

Tammuz: Tammuz is Dammuzi in Sumerian/Akkadian. A Shepherd god. The Canaanite ritual of "mourning for Tammuz" is mentioned in the Book of Ezekiel. Tammuz was probably based on a real person, a Mesopotamian "shepherd king." There are two men named Tammuz on the Sumerian king list. Damuzi the Shepherd King is called Dumuzid of Bab-tibira. He is said to have ruled for 36,000 years and was the fifth king before the great flood. There is also a Dumuzid of Kuara who was the fifth king of the Uruk dynasty and ruled a mere 100 years. There is no connection between Tammuz and Semiramis except that perhaps Semiramis probably worshiped Tammuz, since Tammuz had been deified centuries before her birth. (Semirimis lived in the 800s BC.) Tammuz is the son of Enki, the god of wisdom and of the water, and Sirtur, the sheep goddess in Mesopotamian mythology. The texts telling the story of Tammuz can be read in "Inanna: Queen of Heaven and Earth" by Diane Wolkstein and Samuel Noah Kramer. In the stories it is very clear that Tammuz is a shepherd god. I made him the son of Baal in this story. I was inspired by a translation of the Baal cycle where the heifer Anath conceives the "lord" by Baal. Adonis is a word for lord, and is a Greek god that may (or may not be) loosely based on Tammuz. (Many scholars believe that Adonis is Eshmoun and that the theory that Tammuz is Adonis is an error made by the left-wing extremist Joseph Campbell.) The reason I felt that I had to include Tammuz is because he is mentioned in the Bible and because of the obsession with Tammuz among the "restorationist" cults-who inspired me to do this research and write this story in the first place.

Tanith: Tanith was the patron goddess of Carthage and Numidia. Tanit was worshiped in Punic contexts in the Western Mediterranean, from Malta to Gades into Hellenistic times. She was, as well as a consort of Baal Hammon, a heavenly goddess of war, a mother goddess and nurse, and a symbol of fertility. There is significant, albeit disputed, evidence, both archaeological and within ancient written sources, pointing towards child sacrifice forming part of the worship of Tanit and Baal Hammon.

Watchers: In Apocrypha, the Books of Enoch refer to both good and evil Watchers, with a primary focus on the rebellious ones. In Daniel 4:13, 17, 23 there are three references made to the class of "watcher, holy one" (watcher, Aramaic `iyr, holy one Aramaic *qaddiysh*). In the Aramaic Book of Enoch, the Watchers (Aramaic, *iyrin*), are angels dispatched to Earth to watch over the humans. The Watchers are called *Zopha Shamayim*, meaning "watchers of heaven" in Sanchuniathon.

Yam: The god of the sea. Yam seems to be identified with the Leviathan, a chaos monster that dwells in the waters.

Yarikh: The Canaanite moon-god. His name is found in that of the Biblical city of Jericho. Jerah, Jarah, or Jorah and Yarkhibol in Phoenician) is a moon god in Canaanite religion whose epithets are "illuminator of the heavens'", "illuminator of the myriads of stars" and "lord of the sickle". The latter epithet may come from the appearance of the crescent moon. Yarikh was recognized as the provider of nightly dew, and married to the goddess Nikkal, his moisture causing her orchards to bloom in the desert. In Babylonia, the moon-god was called Sin and we see the name of this god in the place-name Sinai. The Semitic moon god Su'en/Sin is in origin a separate deity from Sumerian Nanna, but from the Akkadian Empire period the two undergo syncretization and are identified. He is commonly designated as *En-zu*, which means "lord of wisdom". During the period (c.2600-2400 BCE) that Ur exercised a large measure of supremacy over the Euphrates valley, Sin was naturally regarded as the head of the pantheon. It is to this period that we must trace such designations of Sin as "father of the gods", "chief of the gods", "creator of all things", and the like. The "wisdom" personified by the moon-god is likewise an expression of the science of astronomy or the practice of astrology, in which the observation of the moon's phases is an important factor. Interestingly, the Moon was believed to be the father of the Sun! His wife was Ningal ("Great Lady"), who bore him Utu/Shamash ("Sun") and Inanna/Ishtar (the goddess of the planet Venus). The tendency to centralize the powers of the universe led to the establishment of the doctrine of a triad consisting of Sin/Nanna and his children. Sin had a beard made of lapis lazuli and rode on a winged bull. The bull was one of his symbols, through his father, Enlil, "Bull of Heaven", along with the crescent and the tripod (which may be a lamp-stand). On cylinder seals, he is represented as an old man with a flowing beard and the crescent symbol. In the astral-theological system he is represented by the number 30 and the moon. This number probably refers to the average number of days (correctly around 29.53) in a lunar month, as measured between successive new moons. Some scholars theorize that El was originally a moon god.

Xoanon: A Xoanon was an archaic wooden cult image of Ancient Greece. Classical Greeks associated such cult objects, whether aniconic or effigy, with the legendary Daedalus. Many such cult images were preserved into historical times, though none have survived to the modern day, except where their image was copied in stone or marble. Xoanon were often a trunk of a tree sometimes with minor crude sculpting. Pausanias noted that "The sanctuary of Athena Chalinitis is by the theater, and near it is a naked *xoanon* of Herakles, said to be by Daidalos. All the works of this artist, though somewhat uncouth to look at, nevertheless have a touch of the divine in them." (*Description*, 2.4.5). A similar practice was found among the ancient Semites with the "Asherah Pole." Many depictions of the "Tree of Life" have been found in Mesopotamian art. We see the practice referred to in the story of Osiris and Isis (De Iside et Osiride by Plutarch) when Isis finds the sacred tree that has engulfed her lover. In **De Dea Syria** ("Concerning the Syrian Goddess") attributed to Lucian of Samosata, the Semitic temple which is described in the visit had a xoanon-most likely the Asherah Pole.

Zadok: Zadok or **Sydyk** (in some manuscripts **Sydek** or **Sedek**) was the name of a deity appearing in a theogeny provided by Roman era Phoenician writer Philo of Byblos in an account preserved by Eusebius in his *Praeparatio Evangelica* and attributed to the still earlier Sanchuniathon. The name probably means "righteousness." Philo of Byblos gave the Greek meaning of the name as *dikaion* i.e. "righteousness" thus indicating that the word corresponds to the West-Semitic root for "righteousness" z-d-q. An Ugaritic reference to a god named Zaduq has also been found, a possible forerunner of Sydyk. Zadok was probably worshiped at "Kittu" by the Babylonians. Zadok is the name of the high priest under King Solomon and the Zadokite priestly lineage descended from him. Some have speculated that as Zadok does not appear in the text of Samuel until after the conquest of Jerusalem, he was actually a Jebusite priest co-opted into the Israelite state religion. Harvard Divinity School Professor Frank Moore Cross refers to this theory as the "Jebusite Hypothesis," criticizes it extensively, but terms it the dominant view among contemporary scholars, in *Canaanite Myth and Hebrew Epic: Essays in the History of the Religion of Israel*. Elsewhere in the Bible, the Jebusites are described in a manner that suggests that they worshipped the same God (El Elyon) as the Israelites, in the case of Melchizedek. Further support for this theory comes from the fact that other Jebusites or residents of pre-Israelite Jerusalem bore names invoking the principle or god Zadok or Zedek (*Tzedek*) (see for example Melchizedek and Adonizedek). Under this theory the Aaronic lineage ascribed to Zadok is a later, anachronistic interpolation

Zaphon: *Zaphon* was the most sacred mountain of the Canaanites. Zaphon is Mount Aqraa in Syria. It was called Mount Cassius in Greek probably referring to the word for "seat" in Semitic languages, as in the Seat of the Gods. According to Isaiah 14:13 the mountain *Zaphon* is the location where the gods assembled. The old Semitic name *Zapānu* was used by the conquering Assyrians in the 8th century BCE and by the Phoenicians. As a prominent peak in the northern part of the Canaanite world, its name was used, for example in Psalm 48, Genesis 13:14 and Deuteronomy 3:27, as a synonym for the direction north. *Tzaphon* is in fact the basic word for "north" in Hebrew, due to the location of the mountain and the relation between the Hebrew and Canaanite languages. According to Ugaritic texts it was the sacred mountain of the storm god

Baal (Baal-Hadad in ancient Canaanite mythology), where his palace was erected of blue lapis and silver and where his lightning overcame the nearby sea (Yam) and Death (Mot) himself. The thunderstorm-gathering mountain was an object of cult itself, and on it dwelt also the goddess Anat. Psalm 48 in the Bible, reads, "Great is the LORD, and greatly to be praised, in the city of our God, in the mountain of His holiness, beautiful in its elevation, the joy of the whole world, like the heights of Zaphon is Mount Zion, the city of the Great King."

Bibliography

You can read the actual Ugaritic texts themselves in English translation. (As opposed to my spin on them which you find in this book.) These stories in direct translations can be read in **"Stories from Ancient Canaan"** edited and translated by Michael David Coogan. There is now **"Stories from Ancient Canaan, Second Edition"** Edited and Translated by Michael D. Coogan and Mark S. Smith. The second edition includes "El's Drinking Party" and "The Lovely Gods." "The Lovely Gods," seems to be a fragmentary creation story. In "The Lovely Gods," El fathers Shachar and Shalim from the goddesses. The second edition updates the book and brings it closer to where Ugaritic scholarship is at today. Coogan also made improvements such as changing the chapter previously entitled "The Healers" to the more accurate "The Rephaim." **"Canaanite Myths and Legends"** by John C. Gibson is also available. Gibson's work has the Ugaritic texts transliterated into English letters with a parallel translation into English. Translation of the texts can also be found in **Ugaritic Narrative Poetry** by Simon B. Parker. **"Dances with the Gods: Canaanite-Phoenician Myths & Legends Retold"** by Wafa Stephan Tarnowski tells the story of Canaanite myths in the form of a children's book. See also **Canaanite Religion: According to the Liturgical Texts of Ugarit** by Gregorio Del Olmo Lete.

The story of Tammuz can be read in **"Inanna: Queen of Heaven and Earth: Her Stories and Hymns from Sumer"** by Diane Wolkstein and Sameul Noah Kramer. Inaana is the name for Ashtoreth/Isthar used in Sumer.

There are Bible Study tools that are very helpful that deal with the "Baal Cycle" and other ancient texts. These include **"Readings from the Ancient Near East: Primary Sources for Old Testament Study"** by Bill T. Arnold and Bryan E. Beyer and **"Old Testament Parallels: Laws and Stories from the Ancient Near East"** by Victor H. Matthews and Don C. Benjamin.

A detailed investigation into the Bible and Canaanite Mythology can be found in **"Yahweh and the Gods and Goddesses of Canaan"** by John Day. I found John Day's book very helpful and a thorough examination of the Bible and Canaanite mythology. An earlier book by the famous Bible scholar, the late William Foxwell Albright is similarly entitled **"Yahweh and the Gods of Canaan: A Historical Analysis of Two Contrasting Faiths."**

Mark S. Smith has written **"The Origins of Biblical Monotheism: Israel's Polytheistic Background and the Ugaritic Texts."** I do not agree with all of his conclusions. However, I like the way he challenges Frazer's "The Golden Bough" with its incorrect notions of dying and rising gods. While there are similarities in these myths of supposed "dying and rising gods" there are also very important differences. I enjoyed reading **"The Birth of Monotheism: The Rise and Disappearance of Yahwism"** by Andre Lemaire and I found this book to be very helpful.

To understand the Canaanites and the Israelites beliefs about the Afterlife you can read Rachel S. Hallote's **"Death, Burial, and the Afterlife in the Biblical World."** To understand the world-view of the ancients I recommend John Gray's **"Near Eastern Mythology"** and **"Ancient Near

Eastern Thought and the Old Testament: Introducing the Conceptual World of the Hebrew Bible" by John H. Walton. John H. Walton has also written **The Lost World of Genesis One: Ancient Cosmology and the Origins Debate** and **Genesis 1 as Ancient Cosmology.**

A survey of Mesopotamian mythology is found in "**Handbook to Life in Ancient Mesopotamia**" by Stephen Bertman.

The Penguin Handbook of Ancient Religions (Penguin Reference Library) by John Hinnells

Since the Canaanite gods were widely worshipped in Egypt and because many were assimilated into the Egyptian pantheon, Richard H. Wilkerson's **The Complete Gods and Goddesses of Ancient Egypt** is a helpful resource for studying Canaanite mythology.

The Goddess Anath: Canaanite Epics on the Patriarchal Age (Texts, Hebrew Translation, Commentary and Introduction) by Umberto Cassuto

Did God Have a Wife?: Archaeology and Folk Religion in Ancient Israel by William G. Dever (In this book, the author is not merely recounting the archeological finding but is advocating what I view as radical feminist ideology.)

Each Man Cried Out to His God: The Specialized Religion of Canaanite and Phoenician Seafarers by Aaron Jed Brody

Phoenician Secrets: Exploring the Ancient Mediterranean by Sanford Holst

Israel's Struggle with the Religions of Canaan by Elmer B. Smick and **Religious Diversity in Ancient Israel and Judah** by John Barton.

The Good and Evil Serpent: How a Universal Symbol became Christianized by James H. Charlesworth

Dictionary of Deities and Demons of the Bible by Karel Van Der Toorn, Bob Becking and Pieter W. Van Der Horst (May 30, 1999)

Carthage Must be Destroyed: The Rise and Fall of an Ancient Civilization by Richard Miles (Viking, 2010)

Carthage by Serge Lancel

"Peoples of the Past"

Canaanites by Jonathon N. Tubb (University of Oklahoma Press, 1998)

Phoenicians by Glenn Markoe (University of California Press, 2000)

"Peoples of the Ancient World"

Carthaginians by Dexter Hoyos (Routledge, London and New York, 2010)

Israelites by Anthony Kamm

Biblical Archeology Review

Edward L. Greenstein "Texts from Ugarit Solve Biblical Puzzles" BAR, November/December 2010

Victor Hurowicz "Solomon's Temple in Context" BAR, March/April 2011

William W. Hallo "The Origin of Israelite Sacrifice" BAR, November/December 2011

Baruch Margalit "Why King Mesha of Moab Sacrifices his Oldest Son"-BAR November/December 1986

Ugaritic Language

Basics of Ancient Ugaritic: A Concise Grammar, Workbook and Lexicon by Michael James Williams

A Primer on Ugaritic: Language, Culture and Literature by William M. Schniedewind and Joel H. Hunt

A Grammar of the Ugaritic Language by Daniel Sivan

A Manuel of Ugaritic by Pierre Bordreuil and Dennis Pardee

An Introduction to Ugaritic by John Huehnergard

A Basic Grammar of Ugaritic Language with Selected Texts and Glossary by Stanislav Segert

Ugarit: Ras Shamra (Cities of the Biblical World) by Adrian Curtis

Ugarit and the Old Testament: The Remarkable Discovery and its impact of Old Testament Studies by Peter C. Craigie

Web-sites

Baalism in Canaanite Religion and Its Relation to Selected Old Testament Texts by Greg Herrick

http://bible.org/article/baalism-canaanite-religion-and-its-relation-selected-old-testament-texts

The Religion of the Canaanites

http://www.theology.edu/canaan.htm

The Obscure Goddess On-line Dictionary

http://www.thaliatook.com/OGOD/phoenician.html

The Gods of Canaan: A Home of the Ancient Gods of Canaan

http://www.godsofcanaan.blogspot.com/

Modern Canaanite Spirituality

Natib Qadish means "The Sacred Path" in Canaanite/Hebrew. Tess Dawson seems to be trying to spear-head a revival of the ancient Canaanite religion under this name. She has written "Whisper of Stone: Natib Qadish: Modern Canaanite Religion," "The Horned Altar," and "Anointed." Her website is www.canaanitepath.com. In her books she notes that it is not desirable to worship exactly like the ancient Canaanite did. She says that Jews and Christians don't worship as they did in ancient times either. As the Jews no longer have a Temple in Jerusalem, that is clearly true, whether or not that is true of Christianity is debatable. She seems to deny that the ancient Canaanites carried out human/infant sacrifice. I think that the Romans exaggerated the extent of child sacrifice among the Canaanite, but I think that the practice was not unknown and although it may have been extremely rare, I believe that it did take place. Scholars debate this, but it seems to me that the predominance of evidence points to rare instances of child sacrifice. She does seem to have done some good research into Canaanite religious practices and beliefs. I believe that the prophets of Yahweh also felt that it was no longer desirable for Israelites to worship in accordance to their ancient Canaanite customs and were endeavoring to reform these practices. Jeremiah, Hosea and Amos looked upon Israel's time in the desert under Moses with nostalgia believing that this was a period before Israel was corrupted by Canaanite practices, but, as we have seen, the Israelites had worshiped Canaanite/Syrian and Egyptian gods during their time in Egypt and were followers of the god El. Moses taught the Israelites that Yahweh was the true El and that they should worship Yahweh alone. (See Amos 2:16, Jeremiah 2:2027 and Amos 5:25.)

Sounds From Silence: Recent Discoveries in Ancient Near Eastern Music

Professor Anne Draffkorn Kilmer and Richard Crocker of the University of California at Berkeley narrate information about ancient near eastern music texts and tuning instructions. "A Hurrian Cult Song from Ancient Ugarit (ca. 1400 B.C.)" is performed on a replicated lyre. The booklet gives excellent translations and discussion of the texts. Also Included are photographs of the Hurrian Hymn tablet, Kilmer's transcription of her arrangement in modern music notation, and many delightful drawings of musicians and instruments from ancient sources in the near east.

A CD and large, 23-page illustrated booklet titled: "Sounds of Silence: Recent Discoveries in Ancient Near Eastern Music." Anne D. Kilmer, Richard L. Crocker and Robert R. Brown, (copyright 1976), is available from BellaRomaMusic.com, or by emailing jcsmith8@pacbell.net.

About the Author

Reverend Stephen Andrew Missick is the author of *The Assyrian Church in the Mongol Empire, Mar Thoma: The Apostolic Foundation of the Assyrian Church in India,* and *Socotra: The Mysterious Island of the Church of the East* which were published in the Journal of Assyrian Academic Studies (Volume XIII, No. 2, 1999, Volume XIV, No. 2, 2000 and Volume XVI No. 1, 2002). (See www.jaas.org.) He is the author of *The Words of Jesus in the Original Aramaic: Discovering the Semitic Roots of Christianity, The Secret of Jabez, Saint Thaddeus and the King of Assyria, The Ascents of James: A Lost Acts of the Apostles, The Hammer of God: The Stories of Judah Maccabee and Charles Martel, The Ennead: The Story of Osiris the Vindicator, the Beloved Enchantress Isis and Horus the Avenger* and *Christ the Man.* He is an ordained minister of the gospel. He graduated from Sam Houston State University and Southwestern Baptist Theological Seminary. Rev. Missick has traveled extensively throughout the Middle East and has lived among the Coptic Christians in Egypt and Aramaic Christians in Syria. He also served as a soldier in Operation Iraqi Freedom in 2003 and 2004. While serving as a soldier in Iraq he learned Aramaic from native Aramaic-speaking Iraqi Assyrian Christians. Rev. Missick is the writer and illustrator of the comic book "The Assyrians: The Oldest Christian People," the comic strip *Chronicles: Facts from the Bible* and the comic book series *The Hammer of God* which are available from www.comixpress.com. *The Hammer of God* comic book series dramatizes the stories of Judah Maccabee and Charles Martel. He has also served as a chaplain in the Army National Guard in Iraq during his second deployment in 2009 and 2010. He participated in an archeological excavation of Bethsaida in Galilee in 2011 and went on a missionary trip to Uganda in 2012 and India in 2013.

PO Box 882, Shepherd, Texas, 77371
BLOG: www.aramaicherald.blogspot.com
YOUTUBE CHANNEL: www.youtube.com/aramaic12

Printed in Great Britain
by Amazon.co.uk, Ltd.,
Marston Gate.